SHERLOCK IN THE SPRING TIME

Some Idle Thoughts on Holmes and Watson

From

Molly Carr

Paperback ISBN 9781780923413
ePub ISBN 9781780923420
PDF ISBN 9781780923437

Published in the UK by MX Publishing
335 Princess Park Manor, Royal Drive, London, N11 3GX

www.mxpublishing.co.uk

Cover design by www.staunch.com

FOR ELIZABETH

Note on the Cover Illustration

Fervid fans of Holmes, and/or sharp-eyed readers, will see that Sherlock is holding a rose, which is hardly a spring-time flower. But the author claims poetic licence.

ILLUSTRATIONS

CONTENTS

The Maiwand Lion

Sheerluck Homes and Doctor Spotson

The Sherlock Holmes Museum Meiringen

Introduction

To study Sherlock Holmes is to go on a long and exciting journey. People the world over recognise his name. Most know he is *the* detective. They are familiar with the deerstalker, the lens and the ulster. But the problem is how to present a book which will interest the general reader without attracting the scorn of those who are obsessive about the man and his doings. For many lovers of the canon *are* obsessive when it comes to playing the 'Grand Game'. Societies exist the world over for ever-eager members, who sometimes seem to think of little else but dressing up as Doyle's characters, visiting the scenes of Sherlock's triumphs (and even his occasional failures) and reading, or even writing, about him.

The most popular tales seem to be those from pseudo-Watsons who copy (as far as they are able) the style and subject matter of the original. Others are pastiches which aren't at all in his style, or even close, but make free use of the characters the Doctor has told us about. Some are stories which bring in characters from other books, and sometimes real-life people as well.

Films have been made from very early days in almost every language. Some are conscientious copies of the canon. Most take liberties with it. Debates rage over who is, or was, the best Sherlock on stage and screen. Nothing has caused more division among fans than the most recent television series and the most recent movies.

Quite as much material has been produced about Doyle. The houses he inhabited and their subsequent fate, what he did before he decided to put pen to paper, how he rescued real-life people accused of real-life crimes, his devotion to spiritualism, his part in the Boer War and his friendships with Oscar Wilde, Harry Houdini, J. M. Barrie and one of Britain's most flamboyant kings, Edward VII, who awarded him a knighthood in the Coronation Honours list of 1902.

These 'thoughts' are the fruit of nearly ten years studying the canon and the life of Conan Doyle, writing two pastiches, a Biography of Doctor Watson and a Sherlock Holmes 'Who's Who': and I hope that in *Sherlock In The Spring Time* readers will find much to entertain, with enough esoteric information to catch the interest of even the most knowledgeable Sherlockian. For those new to the iconic pair, I have tried as far as possible to include material which will tempt them to want to read more about the man and his doings.

Doyle's characters have inspired hundreds of imitations, some good, some very good and some indifferent or, frankly, bad: two men who are household names, written about by professors, clergymen, novelists famous in their own right – and a host of others. So happy Holmesian reading!

A TRIC'KY PROBLEM - EPISODE ONE

Stopping for lunch at a Carvery on the way home from a visit to the American Cemetery at Madingly, near Cambridge, England, wouldn't (I suspect) normally result in a mysterious encounter with Sherlock Holmes.

But the walls of this particular inn were plastered with pictures and artefacts of every kind supplied on a rotating basis by a firm appropriately named 'Elegant Clutter'; and a leisurely look round after the meal revealed a cartoon by someone called 'Tric'. To me, it resembled nothing so much as a not very flattering drawing of Richard Lancelyn Green, a man famous for his interest in all things Holmesian. However, the pipe was there; and a small brass plate bore the legend that it was indeed Sherlock, or at least his head.

Later that week, after reaching home, I wrote to ask for information about this particular piece of 'Clutter', so much out of place with the rest of the decorations, but received no reply. A second letter was also ignored, along with several emails. Somewhat piqued by this, my next step was to send an email to the brewery. This resulted in a courteous letter from the Guest Services Department asking if I could supply a contact number as the manager of the relevant restaurant was suddenly very anxious to get in touch. Contact number naturally supplied, this called forth a friendly telephone call. Did I want to know about something on the wall? The manager of the Carvery would do more than that: remove whatever it was at once and send it to me.

There were at least two reasons for thinking the girl

had done as she said: a pause, and the sound of her high heels clattering away in the distance before she came breathlessly back to the telephone to say that the drawing was now in her office and would be immediately despatched in my direction. Six months later I was still waiting so made another telephone call, which again resulted in profuse apologies but no picture. The restaurant was very busy. My telephone number and address had unfortunately been mislaid, could she have them again, didn't have pencil and paper to write anything down, only that morning she'd discovered the drawing in her room. If it hadn't arrived by Friday (this was Monday) I was to ring again.

    Well it didn't, and I didn't. Instead, thinking nothing was likely to happen after so long, I got in touch with the editor of a prestigious journal, sent out periodically to fellow members of an equally prestigious Sherlockian Society, giving the exact position of the artefact as I had seen it so many months earlier. To my surprise and gratification the President himself went along to find out what *he* could discover. But he was unable to spot Tric (so the cartoon had been taken off the wall?) and was naturally 'reluctant to lean over the other diners and peer at each picture.'

I decided to send an email to 'Elegant Clutter'. Even though they had upwards of 1750 things to choose from when it came to perking up pubs, they should surely know something? The result was the same as when I first contacted the Carvery. Dead silence. So, after licking my wounds for a while, I fired off a salvo in the shape of a postcard to the manager of the said Carvery, saying I didn't think the artefact, an ugly object surrounded by an intricate silver-coloured metal frame of incredible vulgarity and with the addition of the small brass plate already mentioned, was hers to give away. If she cared to send it I would pay postage, inspect the thing at my leisure (and more thoroughly than I had been able to do in the restaurant) photograph and then rapidly return it.

Readers who have come this far will have already guessed what happened next, or rather what didn't, and hasn't, happened next. Perhaps I should have given my address as 221B Baker Street and called myself Doctor Watson.

This, and the piece following, first appeared in 'The Baker Street Bugle', the newsletter of The Deerstalkers of Welshpool -'The only Sherlock Holmes Society in Wales'.

A TRIC'KY PROBLEM - EPISODE TWO

The influence of the Deerstalkers obviously extends far beyond the borders of Welshpool. After more than a year of fruitless letters, emails, telephone calls and enlisting the help of others, the cartoon I wrote about in the March 2011 issue of 'The Baker Street Bugle' arrived by post *less than a month* later – with a message from the manager apologising for "the very long time taken in sending it to you." But did she?

I described the original, which was small, as "an ugly object surrounded by an intricate silver-coloured metal frame of incredible vulgarity, with the addition of a small brass plate." But what came to the house, too big to get through the letter-box, was a large drawing beautifully framed. Were mysterious pictures of the most famous detective in the world proliferating in this particular Carvery, in much the same way as St. Paul's Cathedral? Which, said Sidney Smith when he first saw The Brighton Pavilion, "must have gone down to the sea and pupped"?

Due to the size of the new picture it was possible to see much more detail, including the name of the artist which turned out to be 'Trist' not 'Tric'. This rapidly put paid to a punning title, of course. But the sign-post 'Baker Street', as well as the pipe and the deerstalker, indicated that the subject was meant to be Holmes. There was even a faintly pencilled 'S. H.' on the backing. (Yes, I did take the thing to bits, hunting for clues). Instead of a gold-coloured metal plate, however, there was an insert of identical gothic script on gold-coloured paper.

This tells the reader that "Sir Arthur Conan Doyle's

celebrated detective Sherlock Holmes and his faithful colleague Dr. Watson appeared in over 60 novels and short stories. The character was based on Dr. Joseph Bell, an Edinburgh surgeon under whom Doyle studied medicine. Holmes, in the stories, had a brilliant analytical mind but was addicted to cocaine, prone to fits of depression and played the violin wherever he needed to think!"

But surely Sherlock was too "lynx-eyed"[1] to need glasses? So who was it in reality? When, why and where was the cartoon drawn? At a dinner given by one of the hundreds of societies around the world which meet to honour the Master? At an exciting event when all the members dressed up? On the evidence of the writing with its queer lettering and slightly strange wording (which, however, is in English) did the dinner take place in Germany? Did a German Society entertain a number of British Sherlockians and then decide to brighten things up by employing someone to draw each one of them individually? And who had the brass neck to call Holmes a 'character' when we all know that he's real?

In the manner of many cartoonists the drawing is, as one can see, nearly all head - with body, legs and boots hardly big enough to support it; and there's a most uncharacteristic scarf round Sherlock's neck. Holmes leers (there's no other word for it) through an enormous spy-glass, and bares his teeth in a nasty grin. He's on the trail of somebody, just as I am now on the trail of Trist. If

---

[1] See page 56

14

successful, there may yet be a third episode of A Tric'ky Problem.

MEDITATIONS ON THE MUSGRAVE RITUAL

A number of low budget films starring Basil Rathbone as Holmes and Nigel Bruce as Watson were made throughout the nineteen-forties. For example, *Sherlock Holmes in Washington* sees the pair trying to foil Nazi spies intent on stealing a microfilmed document concealed in a match folder; and *Sherlock Holmes Faces Death,* released in 1943, has a number of weird murders taking place in a convalescent home for retired officers. Nevertheless, film critic Leslie Halliwell says of this latter effort, "It is one of the better entries in this rather likeable modernised series; fairly close to the original story ['The Musgrave Ritual'] except that the events don't make a lot of sense."

But then the story as told to Watson by Holmes for inclusion in *The Strand Magazine* for May 1893 doesn't make much sense either. It's not likely that whole swathes of Musgraves would have to wait for Sherlock to solve a simple riddle: which in any case has already been worked-out before his arrival on the scene by the family butler.

However, as we are told that the man is a former teacher able to speak several languages and play every musical instrument this presumably made him a cut above the common run of servants. As Holmes says to Reginald Musgrave, "Your butler appears to me to have been a very clever man, and to have had a clearer insight than ten generations of his masters." Reginald Musgrave, on the other hand, has never been particularly interested in the Ritual. To him it was only a matter of question and answer, to be learned by heart like a child's catechism once he had come of age.

As it is, the Ritual is, unfortunately, far from perfect. For example, no allowance is made for the fractional changes over the centuries of the sun's position relative to the earth. Nothing is said about the relative growth of the two trees, which is crucial when it comes to trying to solve the puzzle; or even, perhaps, the lack of growth, seeing that one tree, the oak, dates from as long ago as the Norman Conquest. In addition, it's difficult to imagine how the key to finding the first reference point on the treasure trail (the end of the shadow of the elm) could be encoded, and subsequently decoded, unless an assumption is made that it lies in line with both the oak and the elm. Without this assumption it would be necessary to specify not only the date but also the time, rather than simply say the sun is "Over the oak." The exact position of the first reference point on the line is defined by the length of the shadow of the elm, and Holmes has a lot of fun with fishing line and stick constructing similar triangles to compensate for the destruction earlier of the elm by lightning – but which was coincidently measured by Reginald Musgrave as a boy. Just as mysteriously, Brunton has been in the Musgrave's service for so many years he could have found the treasure at any time once he'd solved the puzzle. One feels he wouldn't have had to wait for the help of a gullible female servant either. It's much more likely that he would have got his now deceased wife to help him much earlier. But these observations are by no means the sum of all the puzzles surrounding the Ritual. There were riots throughout the Christian world in 1752, when the change to another calendar caused irate crowds to demand the return of the eleven days of life they thought they had somehow lost. So which calendar should be consulted, the Julian, the Gregorian or both?

According to T. S. Eliot, in a review for *The Criterion* for April 1929, the greatest of all the Sherlock Holmes mysteries is that when we talk of him we invariably fall into the fancy of his existence; and this reality is a quality which struck readers and critics alike from the beginning. In other words, the detective and his foil aren't characters in a series of short stories and novels. To all intents and purposes they are real entities. But, having declared his interest, one must assume that Eliot read Holmes and, from what follows, paid particular attention to The Musgrave Ritual.

In *Murder in the Cathedral,* written in 1935 for The Canterbury Festival, he provides a strange mystery of his own, one which seems unnecessary for such a prominent and prolific poet. Thomas á Becket returns to Canterbury after being an exile in France for seven years and faces a series of tempters. The First Tempter reminds him of all the good times with the King before he was made an Archbishop and began defying his master over Church rights and privileges: "Singing at nightfall, whispering in chambers, /Fires devouring the winter season, /Eating up the darkness, with wit and wine and wisdom."

But it's the Second Tempter who concerns us more here. Musgrave suggests that Holmes run his eye over a copy of some questions and answers concerning the Ritual and, as Holmes says so many years later, "He handed me this very paper which I have here, Watson, and this is the strange catechism to which each Musgrave had to submit when he came to man's estate. I will read you the questions and answers as they stand."

REGINALD MUSGRAVE

Whose was it?
His who is gone.
Who shall have it?
He who will come.
Where was the sun?
Over the oak.
Where was the shadow?
Under the elm.
How was it stepped?
North by ten and by ten, east by five and by five, south by two and by two, west by one and by one, and so under.
What shall we give for it?
All that is ours.
Why should we give it?
For the sake of the trust.

In Eliot's play the Second Tempter reminds the man soon to be murdered of his time as Chancellor, an office he resigned when he became Archbishop of Canterbury, and says how easily such a position could be regained if Thomas would only submit to the King's will: when such "Power obtained leads to glory." His spiritual power is nothing but "earthly perdition." And if he remains "Cabined in Canterbury" he will be nothing more than a "Self-bound Servant of a powerless Pope." The beleaguered Archbishop considers this offer of power and, in a similar series of question and answer to that which we have just seen, asks:

Who shall have it?
He who will come.

What shall be the month?
The last from the first.
What shall we give for it?
Pretence of priestly power.
Why should we give it?
For the power and the glory.

There are lines here which have been borrowed verbatim from the Ritual, but also a strong feeling that the whole style of the thing has been lifted from Doyle. The final sentences "For the sake of the trust" and "For the power and the glory" while not identical resonate strongly with the original.

Surely an example of one great man being helped out by another.

This first appeared in the autumn 2012 issue of The Torr, the Journal of The Poor Folk on the Moor

T. S. BLAKENEY

A lovely small book[1] (10.6 cms x 17.8 cms), most pleasant to handle, came into my possession recently. With beautifully clear print, copious and meticulous footnotes and three appendices, it forms part of Otto Penzler's Sherlock Holmes Library and was published in 1993 by Otto Penzler Books, New York. While one may quarrel with some of its inclusions (Jean Paul Richter appears to be presented on page 14 as two persons) it's reassuring to see some of my own conclusions, arrived at independently, supported by so famous a commentator. How I wish I had read it earlier, if only to find the quotations from the canon which I wanted to use more easily!

[1] *Sherlock Holmes, Fact or Fiction*? First published by John Murray, London, in 1932.

AN OLD CAMPAIGNER

The reader is led to believe that Watson's first investigation with Holmes took place in *A Study in Scarlet*, which allegedly began when a former Sergeant of Marines appeared in Baker Street with a letter from the Scotland Yard Police Inspector Gregson telling all about the 'bad business' in Lauriston Gardens. We know from internal evidence that the date was March 4th, but what year was it? When exactly did Watson get home from India after being wounded in Afghanistan at the Battle of Maiwand and taken to the base Hospital in Peshawar? When, precisely, did he land at Portsmouth Jetty? How long did it take him to "gravitate" to London? He stayed for "some time" at the hotel in the Strand, and it took him "a day or two" to settle into Baker Street once he'd decided to share lodgings with Holmes.

Watson tells us that the regiment he expected to join had already gone through the passes which separate India from Afghanistan and that he eventually met up with it in Kandahar. But according to its Regimental History the Fifth Northumberland Fusiliers were not stationed in South Afghanistan but on the North West Frontier.[1]

A Soldier of the 5th Regiment of Foot (A 'Northumberland Fusilier') 1742

To reach them Watson would have had to travel by rail from Bombay to Delhi (by way of a connection coming up from Calcutta at Allahabad) and then take the Sind, Punjab and Delhi Line to Amritzar, a distance of 300 miles.[2] From Amritzar he would ride in a *dak* shared by other officers along the Grand Trunk Road as far as Peshawar. To remove him from his brigade to the Berkshires meant the long journey back to Bombay, a sea voyage by troopship to Karachi, a train from there to Sibi, becoming part of a horse and camel 'caravan' across the mountains and enduring twelve 'stages' – marches of a hundred miles each – to Quetta, seven to Charman and six more (including going up the Bolan Pass) to Kandahar.

So why go to all that trouble moving our man from

his brigade and sending him to join the 66th Regiment of Foot? Several reasons have been put forward for the change, including the bizarre one that he had syphilis, but it may have been due to something far less suspicious. Unification of the medical department had already begun in England in 1873, but five years later in India was still working on the regimental lines of 1860 when each brigade was responsible for its own casualties. However, according to Surgeon-Major (later Surgeon-General) G. J. H. Evatt M.D., such a system would not work in war time up the Afghan passes due to the narrowness of the defiles and the scattered nature of the troops. When it became known as early as September 1878 that an Expeditionary Force, under the command of Major-General Sir Donald Stewart, was being organised for combat duty in Afghanistan and would shortly march up to Kandahar, a memorandum on how the medical services should be conducted was submitted to the Government. It had two objectives: to prevent wounded men impeding the fighting progress of healthy troops, and to ensure the best distribution of medical personnel and supplies. Doctors would no longer be commissioned into named regiments. Instead the wounded would be looked after in divisional field and base hospitals, with sections for the various corps and designated medical officers in charge; while others were to be stationed closer to the combatants. Duplication of supplies would be avoided, since each regiment would no longer need to indent separately for its own requirements, and the wounded as far as possible be grouped together behind the lines.

After a great deal of correspondence the 'Précis of Field Medical Services' received Governmental sanction on November 8th 1878. Writing twelve years later Surgeon-Major Evatt said, "At the very last moment, that is to say, one week before the Army crossed the frontier, a plan of field hospitals as opposed to regimental hospitals was sanctioned, but no one knew anything whatever of the details of the scheme. In three days and practically in the face of the enemy all medical officers and medical subordinates had to be removed from their regiments to the little understood new creations called field hospitals; to hand over every grain of medicines, instruments, and technical equipment, tents, books, documents, and to give and receive receipts on both sides; and finally to draw from the commissariat, barrack, ordinance, and transport departments the various equipments needed for the same units the very existence of which was unknown outside the medical department. Few doctors knew what a field hospital was, or how to indent for supplies. As a result, it wasn't until nine o'clock in the evening of the day before the advance to Jamrood that tents for the field hospital were drawn from the Peshawar arsenal." [3]

Although Surgeon-Major Evatt was describing what was happening on the North West Frontier, this chaotic situation applied everywhere. At the very moment Watson crossed into Afghanistan medical men were being decommissioned and then swopped between brigades in the field hospitals. It was just his bad luck that his swops were so far apart.

1. *A History of The Northumberland Fusiliers 1674-1902* by H. M. Walker
2. *Railways of India* by J. N. Westwood

3. The Death March through the Khyber Pass in the Afghan Campaign 1878-79. Published in the "Journal of the United Service Institution of India" No. 82, vol x*ix*, 1890

This first appeared in The School Report, the Quarterly Newsletter of The Priory Scholars of Leicester.

THE REAL WATSON?

An officer who got back to England barely four months after the Battle of Maiwand was Surgeon-Major Alexander Francis Preston. He had been badly wounded in the early stages of the fight and, although there were other surgeons in the field, is thought to be the model for Watson. Attached to the 66th Regiment of Foot – the Berkshires – he was, however, considerably older and more experienced than that relatively new recruit: who barely had time to become used to army life before being retired with a wound pension. Which, being of only nine months duration, was expected to tide him over while he looked for gainful employment in civilian life.

Preston, on the other hand, spent time 'at home' on half-pay for as long as it took for him to recover enough from his wounds to return to active service. His Service Record, which from what follows cannot be accepted as wholly reliable, states that he was wounded at Khush-ni-Nahud and a telegram sent to Headquarters to that effect. The same source says that he was again wounded in Kandahar less than a month later. If so, he was extremely unlucky; and it makes it difficult to believe he tended to the wounded throughout the siege of Kandahar, which followed the British defeat.

'Mentioned in Despatches', the List of Commissioned Officers in the British Army merely states that he served in Afghanistan 1878-1880 and was wounded twice, without specifying where, geographically, his injuries were actually incurred. However, Leigh Maxwell (author of *My God-Maiwand!*) says that the Irishman was carried off the field, seriously wounded, early in the action. Later, when an *Enquiry into the Conduct of the Engagement* was set up, every officer was required by The Commander-in-Chief to write an account of the part he played in it. Preston's account is taken from 'Reports and Narratives of the Officers who were Engaged at the Battle of Maiwand, 27th July 1880. Intelligence Branch, Army H.Q. India' and reads:

After my wounds were attended to, I was lying quietly on my stretcher, when all of a sudden the bearers took it up and began running off with it as fast as they could go, shouting as they ran along that the ghazis were upon us. There was a regular stampede of men and animals making off at the best speed that they could. All was in utter confusion, no order of any kind, but everybody doing the utmost possible to save his own life and get out of the way of danger as fast and best as he could. With this object, all the loads had been taken off the baggage animals which were at once appropriated for riding purposes. The ground was, in consequence, covered with camp equipage, boxes of ammunition and treasure, mess-stores, wines and so on. My bearers had not gone far when they deserted me to a man;

and after two other modes of conveyance in which I had been placed that afternoon had failed, I was finally taken up by a horse artillery wagon. All this time the stampede had been going on, and men of all races, horses, camels and bullocks passed in confusion.

During the retreat, the unfortunate Surgeon-Major in his horse artillery wagon had got as far as Ashu-Khan, about ten miles from Kandahar. Here the horses were unharnessed and watered. Whether or not they had had too much to drink, when they were returned to the wagon they appeared unable to move. Preston's narrative continues:

I lay helpless on the wagon for, I should say, a couple of hours expecting at every moment that some of our party would be shot as the villagers here, as they did all along the road, kept continually firing at us. However, as a few stragglers of the 66th came up, I asked them to stay by me, and use their rifles in return. In this way the villagers were kept off. After some time, a camel with a pair of kajawas came up with Apothecary Cordiero of the Subordinate Medical Department (Bombay), who had been walking all night. He stopped the camel, and had me put in one of the kajawas, and regardless of his own safety remained with me for a long time and did everything in his power to assist me. I had not proceeded far in the kajawa before the cords holding it together commenced to give way, and to save me from falling the camel had to be made to lie down quickly. While lying helpless on the ground in the broken kajawa, I was passed by a large body of Sind Horse...After I had been lying on the ground for some time, Captain Slade of the RHA came up with one of his smooth-bore guns, and seeing me, and the situation I was in at once determined on endeavouring to save my life, and not to leave me to my inevitable fate. His horses were so utterly beaten that they would not have been equal to my additional weight; so in order to save my life he abandoned the gun and had me put upon the limber. Even then it was only by his splendid management and his presence of mind and great coolness in danger (for the inhabitants kept firing at us all along) that he succeeded in getting his horses to move at all.

A kajawa was a hybrid framework part pannier, part stretcher, lashed one each side of a camel's hump. It would have been less than comfortable for a fit man; but for a wounded man the rolling movement of the animal must have made it excruciating.

Preston was later (as a Returning Officer at Portsmouth) reprimanded for sending on troops inadequately provided for. But, unlike Dr. Watson, he recovered enough from his wounds to rejoin his corps and later served in China. It was at this juncture at Maiwand, however, that Gunner J. Hollis earned the Victoria Cross by running in front of the limber and drawing the Afghans' fire away from the gun carriage towards himself. He later left the army, joined the Bombay Police Force, committed bigamy and had his Victoria Cross taken away from him 'For conduct likely to bring it into disrepute'. Many years later, George V changed the rules. He decreed that "A man should keep his medal even if he is on his way to the Scaffold."

Sgt. Mulvane of the Royal Horse Artillery was also at the Battle of Maiwand and earned the Victoria Cross for rescuing a gunner – making him, like Hollis, a possible model for Watson's orderly, Murray. The Battleground was entirely in disarray and there were a large number of horses which had lost their riders and could be grabbed during the rout to carry away a wounded man.

Doyle had the opportunity to meet many badly injured soldiers from all parts of the Empire, including Preston, soon after he arrived in Southsea. He writes in *Memories and Adventures* published by John Murray in 1924 that, in 1882, "A new wave of medical experience came to me about this time for I suddenly found myself a unit in the British Army. The operations in the East had drained the Medical Service and it had therefore been determined that local civilian doctors should be enrolled for temporary duty of some hours a day."

Doyle, unlike some of the other doctors in the area, said at his interview that he would do "anything" and was appointed at once by the Principal Medical Officer responsible for Her Majesty's Forces in India. He went on to describe his temporary boss as "A savage-looking medico who proved to be Sir Alexander Home, V. C. – an honour which he had won in the Indian Mutiny. He was in supreme charge and, as he was fierce in speech and in act as in appearance, everyone was terrified of him..."

However, an entry in Home's diary for 13th October 1857, when he was only thirty-one and known simply as a regimental surgeon, rather belies this fierceness. "The wounded are doing very badly – many are dying of lock-jaw – the most horrible death I know. The honours and rewards of the leaders of armies are certainly purchased by incredible suffering by those under them." Three days later he wrote "It is very painful to get such a [mortally wounded] case into Hospital – to know that the man must eventually die and yet be pretending to do him good." It was Home who recommended Private McManus of the Northumberland Fusiliers (the regiment Watson says he joined on his arrival in Afghanistan) for the V. C.

Conan Doyle worked at Netley until shortly before 1885. By then the situation had eased and all civilian doctors were released from their obligations. But there is no doubt he gained valuable knowledge of military matters, which he was later to use to good effect in his first crime novel. Fourteen years after his marriage to his first wife Louise Hawkins, by which time he had given up medicine to become an established writer, he was visited by the American actor William Gillette who wanted Doyle's approval of his play about Holmes and permission to stage it in the U.S.A. Doyle was living with his family at a house which he had built for Louise and called 'Undershaw'. From there he went to meet Gillette at the nearest station, Haslemere.

It is said by John Dickson Carr in his *Life of Sir Arthur Conan Doyle*, first published by John Murray in 1954, that when the American stepped out of the train Doyle looked at him and saw Sherlock. Gillette, in his turn, looked at Doyle and saw Watson. Was this because Gillette was thinking of Sidney Paget's drawings for *The Strand Magazine*? Or did he have a picture of the man in his mind from reading the *Adventures*? Drawings of Watson by this artist (who had many other commissions, for example drawing King

Edward's belated Coronation Procession for *The Illustrated London News* in 1902) were apparently not modelled on Doyle but on one of Paget's fellow students at Art School, Alfred Morris Butler. Butler, however, *did* resemble Doyle; and Paget's studio portrait of Doctor Doyle, though rather stiff, looks a little like him. Somewhat wary about the eyes instead of the genial sparkle one somehow expects from Watson, Doyle self-consciously fills the frame, his thick moustache hiding his mouth. The very picture of a man determined not to give anything away but afraid that he might.

AMMUNITION BOOTS

In 'The Greek Interpreter' Sherlock Holmes and his brother Mycroft sit in The Strangers' Room of the Diogenes Club, at a bow window overlooking Pall Mall, and indulge in the delightful game of impressing Watson. One of the men coming towards them is, among other things, a non-commissioned army officer who has been in India. He hasn't 'the cavalry stride', but has served in the Royal Artillery and is still wearing his 'ammunition boots'. Has Mycroft seen and heard, or rather not heard, something? Did he notice that the old soldier walked quietly? Because of the danger of accidental sparks setting fire to explosives, ammunition boots were sewn together with no cleats or nails in them.

According to the Principal Medical Officer who accompanied Lieutenant-General Sir Fredrick Roberts and his Field Force on the march from Kabul to Kandahar to relieve the Garrison after the battle of Maiwand (at which Watson says he was so badly wounded), such foot-ware was made of raw material of very indifferent workmanship, lost shape and turned over at the heels after a few days marching and "simply impeded progress". Does 'raw material' mean untreated leather, and could the boots have been a different colour from those worn by the men of other regiments? Mycroft implies that everything is being deduced visually.

The P.M.O. with Roberts said that "The Little Ghurkha, who is very fond of the British soldier, invariably adopts the ammunition boot, but as his foot occupies about half the boot I do not think he is the gainer by the transaction." However, one of the advantages of leather is that the wearers don't acquire electrical charges of sufficient energy to cause a spark. The synthetic rubber used for boots in later years needed to be in specially formulated compounds with electrically conducting carbon-black in order to match the former advantages of leather.

This piece, and Doyle on Doyle (1), *first appeared in The School Report.*

ON BEING VERY WELL-KNOWN

"I hear of Sherlock everywhere," says Mycroft Holmes in 'The Greek Interpreter'. And so do I. From F. E. Benson to John Buchan, and even P. G. Wodehouse in *Do Butlers Burgle Banks?* Holmes gets a mention in a number of his other hilarious books too. For example, *Cocktail Time, Jeeves and the Feudal Spirit* and *Much Obliged,*

Jeeves.

There are references to Holmes in Ngaio Marsh's detective novels, as well as those of G. K. Chesterton, Dorothy L. Sayers and many others including, somewhat surprisingly, the now almost unknown Osbert Sitwell, who says the *Adventures* have "that sense of truth to an epoch that memorably distinguishes several books." And any character, whatever his name, who keeps company with a fictional detective for any length of time is likely to be called 'a Watson' or 'my Watson' at least once during the proceedings.

It all began with Conan Doyle's brother-in-law E.W. ('Willie') Hornung who created Raffles the gentleman burglar. He made one joke which delighted Doyle, about a runner who was said by a newspaper to have completed a race in an impossibly short time: "It must be a sprinter's error." But he said of Sherlock "Though he might be more humble, there is no police like Holmes."

Or could it have been J. M. Barrie who started the ball rolling by sending Doyle a Sherlockian Christmas card? Michael Cox, in *Victorian Detective Stories* published as a paperback in 1993, says "Throughout the 1890s and into the early twentieth century the short detective story could not rid itself of Baker Street. In many cases, at least to begin with, it had no wish to do so: public appetite appeared to be insatiable and there was no shortage of publishers to supply it."

In *The Real World of Sherlock Holmes* Peter Costello says about Agatha Christie "She owed him [Conan Doyle] a great deal. After all, Poirot and Hastings are based on Holmes and Watson; her use of detail owes much to

Watson; and both had written books on and about Dartmoor." Hastings (called by Emma Lathen "An all-purpose stooge") has, like Watson, been invalided out of the services. He is given a war pension for a short time and has spent a few "depressing months" in a convalescent home. At a loose end, he tells a friend (in *The Mysterious Affair at Styles*) "I've always had a hankering to be a detective." The friend asks if he means Sherlock Holmes or…? Hastings' reply to this is "Oh, Sherlock Holmes by all means. But really, seriously, I'm awfully drawn to it."

However, my favourite reference of all comes from a character in *Grey Mask* by Patricia Wentworth, who says of her detective Maud Silver, like Miss Jane Marple a compulsive knitter, "She has old Sherlock boiled!"

THE ROYAL VICTORIA MILITARY HOSPITAL

Watson tells us that, after finishing his studies at Bart's and obtaining the degree of Doctor of Medicine from the University of London, he "proceeded to Netley to go through the course prescribed for surgeons in the Army." This normally lasted about six months, with some time spent doing military training at the Army Barracks in Aldershot. The photograph below shows the Chapel, which is all that remains of the Hospital in what is now the Royal Victoria Park.

REFINING THE SEARCH

It isn't clear when Watson decided to share lodgings with Holmes or how long it was before *A Study in Scarlet* intervened, an investigation which was to set the pattern of his existence for some time to come. The unfortunate Doctor, if he *was* sent to the wrong Base Hospital, may have spent even more time in Peshawar trying to recover his health than we thought. He may not have arrived in England until more than a year after the Battle of Maiwand, which took place on July 27th 1880, between a British Force and one led by Ayub Khan, the Governor of Herat Province and brother of the Amir of Afghanistan.

Having unexpectedly won this Battle, and inflicted great losses on British and Indian troops, Ayub and his Army then laid siege to Kandahar. This, of course, would mean that no troops (wounded or otherwise) could be evacuated from that city until Major-General Roberts arrived from Kabul with a relieving force. Even so, the journey to Peshawar for a wounded Watson would be time-consuming and extremely hazardous, as well as decidedly uncomfortable. And, just as he is recovering from his injuries, the poor man tells us he was struck down by the extremely dangerous enteric fever, from which few combatants, already weakened by campaigns, ever recovered. So can the plaque on a wall near the Pathology Laboratory at Bart's, which reads 'At this place New Year's Day 1881 were spoken these deathless words "You have been in Afghanistan, I perceive," by Mr Sherlock Holmes in greeting to John H. Watson at their first meeting', be correct?

There has been some confusion about the actual date on which the battle of Maiwand took place. Jack Tracy, in his admirable *Encyclopaedia Sherlockiana* (Avon, 1979), opts for the twenty-seventh of June (as does June Thomson in her interesting *The Secret Journals of Sherlock Holmes*). But this is obviously a mistake. Other sources mention men returning from hostilities on the *morning* of July 27th, confusing them with General Burrows' reconnoitring force sent out the day before. The Court Circular published in *The Times* for August 18th 1882 records the date as 24th July 1880.

However, Major-General Frederick Roberts' reprisal with Ayub Khan's Army took place on September 1st, after the former had arrived in Kandahar from Kabul with his Relief Force at the end of August. Taking these dates – July 27th and September 1st 1880 – as a starting point, Watson couldn't have made up his mind to change his way of life as early as the commonly accepted date. He says of his stay in hospital that he only rallied enough to walk about the wards and to bask a little on the verandah before being struck down by the fever already mentioned, in which case he was (as noted earlier) lucky to be alive at all. The area around Peshawar was known to European troops as the valley of death, and those who went there couldn't wait to leave. Either the Doctor has exaggerated the length of his illness, his period of recovery or his stays at various venues before being introduced to Holmes, or the supposed date of their meeting should be considerably advanced.

Even if we accept that he muddled up the names of the base hospitals and *was* one of the eighteen invalids who left Karachi in the *Orontes* roughly six weeks after the Kandahar Garrison was relieved by Roberts and arrived in England in November 1880, he would still have to go some to meet Sherlock on the first day of January 1881. For example, how long after he docked at Portsmouth Jetty did he stay in Hampshire? 'Gravitating' to London implies a period of doubt about what to do next, and his "comfortless, meaningless existence" in the hotel in the Strand lasted for quite a while. It is only when he realises that he is living beyond his means, and feels the need to retrench, that he uses the word "soon". And even healthy combatants who took part in the Battle of Maiwand didn't get back to barracks in Britain until February 18th, 1881.

However, it makes for better 'theatre' to fix the famous meeting for New Year's Day. The laboratories were empty, apart from Sherlock, and the streets thronged with people. January 1st didn't become a bank holiday until 1971, and in the nineteenth century most people worked on Saturday mornings, even professionals. Was 'young Stamford' on his way out to lunch after finishing a morning's stint as a newly qualified doctor at Bart's when he met Watson? Were the streets crowded with Saturday afternoon shoppers?

For anyone who thinks, in the light of all Watson's difficulties as a soldier and as a civilian, that it is more likely he met Holmes a year later than he said, it is useful to know that in 1882 January 1st fell on a Sunday. Sherlock, when the mood for action was on him, wouldn't care what day, or what time of day, it was, and may have obtained permission to conduct his own private enquiries into cadavers and/or blood stains on a Sunday as much as a

Saturday afternoon. This permission, once Holmes was accepted as a visitor, would not be difficult to get. Whichever it was, Watson moved out of his hotel "that very evening" and Holmes joined him the following morning.

It took a short time for the two men to arrange their possessions. But in Watson's words they *gradually* adapted to their new life. There were many occasions when Holmes worked hard at something mysterious. But for *days on end* there were "intervals of torpor" when he lay on the sofa not uttering a word or moving a muscle. *Weeks went by* as Watson, whose health forbade him venturing out "unless the weather were exceptionally genial" wondered what Sherlock could be doing for a living. Taken with all the other imponderables, the weather's keeping Watson in points to the season being winter; but fixing his meeting with Holmes for the first day of 1881 allows very little flexibility when trying to sort out a timetable for him after Maiwand.

Dating this first adventure, however, is difficult for other reasons. In 1881 March 4th fell on Friday. But Watson quotes a newspaper as saying that Drebber and Stangerson "bade adieu to their landlady upon *Tuesday, the 4*[th] *inst.*" [My italics] They were last seen later that evening standing on the platform at Euston Station waiting for a late train to Liverpool. The note from Gregson delivered to Holmes by the retired Sergeant of Marines says Drebber's body was discovered at 2 o'clock the next morning. Lestrade finds Stangerson's body in Halliday's Private Hotel, Little George Street, six hours later, but further complicates matters by saying that the two Americans were seen at Euston on *Monday*, March 3rd. Both the newspaper and

Lestrade must be wrong. March 4th fell on a Tuesday in 1884 (a leap year) and on Monday in 1890. It's as if Watson delayed writing up the investigation until 1885 and used last year's calendar (still hanging on the wall) to date it!

To make matters worse, when Holmes and Watson leave Lauriston Gardens after viewing Drebber's corpse, Holmes tells Watson he is in a hurry to get to a concert. He is anxious to hear the famous violinist Wilma Norman-Neruda [Mrs. Charles Hallé]. But Madame Norman-Neruda gave recitals only on Monday evenings and Saturday afternoons. Her concert on Saturday the fifth of March 1881 was the last of the season, starting as usual at 3 p.m.

In 'The Resident Patient' Watson says that he can't be sure of the exact date when this particular investigation was under way, but that it must have been towards the end of the first year he shared lodgings with Holmes. He mentions "boisterous October weather" and, with his "shaken health" being afraid "to face the keen autumn wind." He did not meet Holmes until much later than New Year's Day, 1881. His first year in Baker Street began towards the end of 1881, the Enoch Drebber affair took place five months later, in 1882, and poor Watson was still feeling the effect of his wounds seven months after that. He says of 'The Speckled Band' that the investigation took place at the beginning of April 1883, "in the early days of my association with Holmes, when we were sharing rooms as bachelors." This also implies that he took up lodgings in Baker Street considerably later than January 1st 1881 and affects the chronology of the entire canon.

EXCERPT

Taken from *The Strand Magazine*, vol X, July to December 1895.

'Mr. Conan Doyle has written a powerful Story which will succeed "Brigadier Gerard" in THE STRAND MAGAZINE, commencing with the January Number. It will be entitled "Rodney Stone," and will treat mainly of the period of George III, in a manner which has not hitherto been attempted. Though each instalment will, like "The Adventures of Sherlock Holmes" and "Brigadier Gerard," have separate incidents of its own, there will be a plot running through them all, and the publication of this important work will continue through the greater part of next year.'

Many people know that in 1891 *The Strand* was a new magazine founded by George Newnes. But it may come as a surprise that the first contribution (un-credited) from Conan Doyle (which appeared in the third issue) had little to do with Sherlock Holmes and was called 'The Voice of Science'. British magazines at the time were at a low ebb. They couldn't compete with the more lively American journals, for example *Scribners*; and it was a godsend when that same Doyle turned up at the editorial office later with 'A Scandal in Bohemia' and 'The Red-Headed League.' These, and the rest of Sherlock's Adventures, made the magazine exceptionally popular for many years to come. The two-hundredth issue was published in August 1907 and, by the following month, it was calculated that 80,000,000 copies had been sold since the magazine began. Before that, 'a distressing December issue' caused a public outcry. Holmes had been hurled to his death at the Reichenbach Falls. His creator, however, was persuaded by popular demand, and a very large fee for those days, to bring him back, and Doyle's last story about Holmes appeared in *The Strand* as late as 1927.

Newnes decided there should be at least one picture on every page and that his new venture would sell for sixpence. The number of advertising pages (which never appeared in the six-monthly bound copies) often outstripped those dealing with stories and articles but were essential in covering the cost of production. This was considerable since pictures alone could cost two or three shillings each. However, *The Strand* without photographs was unthinkable – just as *The Strand* without Holmes was to be.

TAKE YOUR PICK

"Holmes was a drug addict without a single amiable trait" – George Bernard Shaw

"Sherlock Holmes is the W. G. Grace of the detective story" - Julian Symonds

WATSON'S RAILWAY JOURNEYS

"Have you a couple of days to spare? Have just been wired for from the West of England in connection with Boscombe Valley tragedy. Shall be glad if you will come with me. Air and scenery perfect. Leave Paddington by the 11.15."

Standing outside his house, complete with a hastily packed valise, one blast of the whistle carried in every gentleman's waistcoat pocket will bring Watson a four-wheeler, and two a hansom. This time, his first recorded railway journey with Holmes, they are off together to Hereford - in a carriage to themselves probably obtained by heavily tipping the guard – and Holmes will occupy part of the time reading newspapers, scattering them over the floor before rolling them into a ball and throwing it onto the luggage rack after the train has passed Reading. The date is between 1889 and 1894, and the train, as already indicated in Sherlock's telegram, is the 11.15 to the West Country, in this case Gloucester and thence to Ross-on-Wye. Watson doesn't mention a change of train, but one was probably necessary. If not, the carriage he shared with Holmes could be uncoupled from the Express and attached to a local train. Or, perhaps with another carriage or two added, *become* the local train.

A lunch stop is to be made at Swindon. This was unavoidable before 1895 because the Great Western Railway (the G.W.R.) had a contract with a catering firm which obliged it to stop every one of its trains there for at least twenty minutes. Such an arrangement was not uncommon. Charles Dickens wrote in *The Uncommercial Traveller*: "You are going off by railway, from any Terminus. You have twenty minutes for dinner before you go." But after 1895 the G.W.R. bought out the catering firm which supplied meals for its passengers and could in future plan where and when, and for how long, its trains stopped.

Holmes gives Watson a run-down of the case, but then retires behind his 'pocket Petrarch' for the rest of the journey. Was the Doctor bored? He says, "It was nearly four o'clock when we at last, after passing through the beautiful Stroud Valley and over the broad, gleaming Severn, found ourselves at the pretty little country town of Ross." This sounds like a real observation. Conan Doyle travelled the Stroud valley route in 1885, crossing the Severn just before Gloucester on his way to Monmouth, a town nine miles from Ross. The purpose of his journey, taken with his future mother-in-law, was to draw up a marriage settlement prior to his wedding with his first wife, Louise Hawkins. Lestrade, who has met Holmes and Watson at the station in Ross, takes the pair to 'The Hereford Arms'. But Holmes is reluctant to travel to Boscombe Valley and the murder scene that evening. He prefers to inspect it the following day. Instead, he goes with Lestrade to Hereford County Gaol to interview the younger McCarthy, a prime suspect in 'The Boscombe Valley Mystery'.

Built in 1793 to replace an older gaol, it was designed by no less an architect than John Nash "on thoroughly modern principles," which included solitary confinement, put forward by the reformer John Howard. It would be knocked down in 1929 to make room for a cinema and a bus station, of which only the bus station now remains, and the male prisoners sent to serve out the rest of their sentences in Gloucester. Female prisoners, however, were sent to Birmingham.

Watson, after seeing their train off, is left alone to amuse himself in Ross, and says that he lay upon the sofa and tried to interest himself in a yellow-backed novel. "The puny plot of the story was so thin, however, when compared with the deep mystery through which we were groping, and I found my attention wander so continually from the fiction to the fact, that I at last flung it across the room."

Other investigations involving journeys to and from Paddington Station are 'The Engineer's Thumb' and 'The Stockbroker's Clerk'. But in 'Silver Blaze', although the pair leave London from Paddington, they later travel back to Waterloo Station from Winchester. In *The Hound of the Baskervilles* the two men also quit London by way of Paddington, as they do in the investigations into 'The Devil's Foot' and 'The Veiled Lodger.'

'A Study in Scarlet', The Stockbroker's Clerk' and 'The Three Garridebs' all involve journeys from Euston, and at least six of their investigations require journeys from or to Waterloo. In 'The Musgrave Ritual' Sherlock travels either from Waterloo or Victoria, while 'The Norwood Builder' and 'The Cardboard Box' mean going from London Bridge. As does 'The Greek Interpreter' and 'The Retired Colourman.'

The most famous (or, perhaps, infamous) journey, which starts from Victoria with Watson trying to turn Holmes – disguised as 'an old Italian priest' – out of the railway carriage, is described in considerable detail in 'The

'I TRIED TO INTEREST MYSELF IN A YELLOW-BACKED NOVEL.'

Final Problem'. But that station must also have been used in 'The Reigate Squire', 'The Golden Pince-Nez', 'The Disappearance of Lady Frances Carfax', 'The Sussex Vampire', 'The Lion's Mane' and maybe in 'Wisteria Lodge'. 'The Gloria Scott' and 'The Dancing Men' both involve train journeys from Liverpool Street.

The following (necessarily incomplete) information about train journeys referred to in the canon may be of interest to those fans of Sherlock Holmes who also love railways. It doesn't pretend to be exhaustive. Neither are the investigations in chronological order, nor yet in order of importance. But, given that Watson 'goes to town' (no pun intended) in some instances and is reticent in others, it's still possible to piece together something of his experiences 'on the line'. And, after all, isn't he equally cagey about other details of his 'adventures' – at the same time as he's quite verbose when it suits him or, more likely, the editor of *The Strand* when short of material to fill a space.

In 'The Stockbroker's Clerk' Holmes and Watson, using assumed names, travel from Euston Station to Birmingham. 'The Engineer's Thumb' has them again leaving Paddington Station, this time to travel to Reading General and then on to 'Eyeford' which may have been the then small town of Early, or perhaps Swindlesham. To get to 'The Copper Beeches' the pair went to Waterloo Station to catch the '9.30', arriving in Winchester two hours later at 11.30 a.m.: and 'The Crooked Man' saw them again at Waterloo to catch the '11.10' to Aldershot. In the gruesome tale involving a 'Cardboard Box', Watson and Holmes could have left London either from London Bridge or Charing Cross Stations on their way to Croydon, and they would use the former Station when travelling to Norwood to deal with that vindictive Builder. 'The Greek Interpreter' has them entraining from London Bridge again, on the '9.45 p.m.' to Beckenham, arriving at Beckenham (East?) three-quarters of an hour later.

Hereford County Gaol before 1929

Would Watson go from Waterloo or Victoria to Hurlestone to find out what was behind 'The Musgrave Ritual'; and to Reigate from the latter to unmask that Squire and his manipulative son? In 'The Sussex Vampire', was it the '2.00' from *Victoria* to 'Lamberley' which, since it's a town "south of   Horsham," could be Watson-speak for Amberley? The two men may also have gone from the same station to Forest Row in 'Black Peter'. Considering the speculative nature of some of these remarks, the relatively precise details of the train journeys in 'The Boscombe Valley Mystery' are rather refreshing!

Could this be 'Boscombe Pool'?
(A photograph of Lough Pool at Sellack near Hereford)

ON PERFORMING SELFISH ACTS

Conan Doyle always maintained that he preferred his historical writing to his other tales. So, in spite of what eventually happened, I have always thought of *A Study in Scarlet* as a one-off which Doyle eventually sold outright to Samuel Beeton for £25. But the tale caught the eye of the editor of the transatlantic *Lippincott's Monthly Magazine* (presumably when it appeared in *Beeton's Christmas Annual)*, and the author resurrected the two main characters for another story which eventually .appeared in the American magazine for February, 1890. That investigation, too, could have stood alone as another one-off for the American market if the British publisher, George Newnes, hadn't started *The Strand Magazine.* Doyle's Literary Agent, A. P. Watt, saw the new periodical as a perfect vehicle for a series of self-contained stories featuring the same two protagonists. But if *The Sign of Four* had also been a single detective story with no follow up, Doyle wouldn't have got himself into such a pickle by marrying Mary Morstan to John H. Watson.

As it is, the year when the couple tied the knot has been argued over interminably. Was it 1887, 1888 or even 1889? During her consultation with Sherlock Holmes, Mary produces a flat jewel case containing six pearls, each of which has been coming to her annually in its own small cardboard box since the beginning of May, 1882. Counting 1882 as the year when the first pearl arrived, and adding the number five, it would seem Miss Morstan first visited Baker Street in 1887. If so, allowing for the time it took to solve the mystery of *The Sign of Four*, to dispose of the Andaman Islander, apprehend Jonathan Small, and allow Watson to overcome his scruples, hers must have been one of the quickest courtships and marriages on record – with a special licence from the Archbishop of Canterbury. This is especially so as, from internal evidence, she first saw Watson as late as July of that year.

Watson says the same year furnished him with a number of investigations of greater or less interest and that one of them, *The Five Orange Pips,* began in the latter days of September, when his wife was on a visit to her mother's. Is his account to be trusted? In *The Sign of Four* Mary had told him (and Holmes) that after her father, Major Morstan, died she was an orphan. In *The Noble Bachelor* Watson writes that the Lord St. Simon marriage took place a few weeks before his own, when he was still sharing lodgings with Holmes but unable to go out because of "high autumnal winds." Again, internal evidence shows that the American heiress, Hatty Doran, received a note from her real husband (causing her to run away during the wedding reception) at the beginning of October. So how could Watson have been married by the previous September? Perhaps he misread his manuscript – doctors have, or did have before the days of computers, a reputation for not writing legibly – and got married in December 1887, thus moving the investigation of *The Five Orange Pips* forward by a couple of months. But it's strange that Mary was away so soon after the wedding.

In *A Scandal in Bohemia* Watson visits Holmes on the 20th of March 1888, saying that his "own complete happiness" as a married man has caused him to see little of his friend lately, quite in order if he did marry towards the end of 1887. His state of euphoria, however, doesn't prevent him from staying the night in his old billet. Two more stories followed: 'The Red-Headed League' and 'A Case of Identity', which was in fact written first and thus follows on from 'A Scandal in Bohemia'. In it Holmes remarks that he hasn't seen his friend for some weeks. In both instances Watson says he called on Holmes at *"his* lodgings"*. No wife is mentioned in the second story in either case, but the inference is that Watson was no longer living in Baker Street. Just as in 'The Blue Carbuncle', where he calls on Holmes just after Christmas to wish him the compliments of the season. Nevertheless, when Holmes remarks in 'The Red-Headed League', before the long vigil in the bank vault, that no doubt the Doctor would like to go home the reply is a somewhat half-hearted "It would be as well." And, after John Clay's capture, the fact that Watson has a wife doesn't prevent the two chums sitting over glasses of whisky and soda in the early hours of the morning while Sherlock wraps up the investigation.

Mary Watson gets to say a few words in her husband's account of 'The Boscombe Valley Mystery', if only to show how very understanding she is, immediately telling her husband in response to a telegram from Holmes that he looks peaky enough to benefit from a few days in the country, even if it means leaving her at home. In 'The Man with the Twisted Lip' she actually acquires a friend and a few more sentences.

In the investigation into the gruesome affair of 'The Engineer's Thumb', which takes place in the summer of 1889, Watson is back to "not *long* after my marriage." He must have been very happy indeed if he did marry in December '87 and the time passed so quickly. In 'The Crooked Man' he tells us that it was "One summer night a few months after my marriage." Unfortunately there is no indication of the year. In 'The Naval Treaty' Watson says that in the July which immediately succeeded his marriage his wife agreed with him that no time should be lost in consulting Holmes about the disappearance of an important State Document. So did that investigation take place soon after 'A Scandal in Bohemia' and 'A Case of Identity'? A busy year indeed! But Doyle couldn't keep up this pretence of a wife. Perhaps the editor of *The Strand Magazine* (Greenhaugh Smith) preferred him not to. Readers were happier with two men regularly battling it out against crime. A wife only got in the way: and there are a number of investigations which supposedly took place before John met Mary, and even two before Holmes met Watson.

Introducing Mary Morstan in *The Sign of Four* romanticises the story and humanises Watson, but left Doyle wondering what on earth to do with her (and sometimes forgetting what to do with her) whenever her husband was required to go off with Holmes. We've seen how she visits her mother, until the author suddenly remembers he made her an orphan and amends this (in 'The Final Problem') to she is (most opportunely) "away on a visit." But in the end it became more convenient to kill the woman off and restore the status quo by getting Watson back into Baker Street. So why bring in another marital mystery about Watson in a story Holmes wrote up for himself called 'The Blanched Soldier'?

THE BEVERLEY MINSTER MYSTERY

While many people may acknowledge that it's pleasant to get into print, there is some danger in doing so. The more exposure, the more unwelcome the consequences may be. So why did Watson write so incautiously and so frequently for the *Strand*? Doubts were cast on his medical ability by Sherlock Holmes in *The Dying Detective*; and Sagittarius, writing in *The London Mystery Magazine* for 1949, said there was one "unsolved mystery" – the case of the strange M.D: "Was he ever qualified? Had he anything to hide? And why was he always free?" Researchers had failed to find out the facts of his previous history and "There was something queer in his medical career, for he never had a single case."

This last was poetic licence for, unless Watson *is* an accomplished liar, we know he treated a railwayman for 'itch-mite' [probably scabies] and Vincent Hatherley for a severed digit in 'The Engineer's Thumb.' And he made valiant efforts to patch up Baron Gruner after that vitriol-throwing incident in 'The Illustrious Client'. But readers of the canon will be aware that he also wrote about the Duke of Holdernesse ('The Priory School') whose seat appears to be in Derbyshire. However Holderness, without the final 'e', is an area in East Yorkshire and the home of the huge cathedral-like church known as Beverley Minster.

The Duke has the courtesy title 'Baron Beverley' and, in the South Aisle of the Nave, a memorial which might have been the Doctor's undoing records the names of thirty three men serving in Afghanistan in 1880 who died marching up from Quetta to relieve Kandahar, under siege by Ayub Khan and his victorious Afghans immediately after the battle of Maiwand. The men belonged to a regiment which Watson never mentions: The 15th of Foot ("The East Yorkshires") – who in any case were beaten to it by Major-General Frederick Roberts and his mixed force from Kabul, which finally lifted the siege at the beginning of September.

But several names later used by Watson appear on the white marble wall tablet. For example: Jackson ('The Crooked Man'), Gibson ('The Problem of Thor Bridge), Smith ('The Solitary Cyclist'), Paterson (original Patterson) casually mentioned in 'The Five Orange Pips' ("The Grice Patersons on the Island of Uffa"), Peterson ('The Blue Carbuncle) and Inspector Patterson ('The Final Problem'). George Burnell, original George Burnett, is the aristocratic villain in 'The Beryl Coronet'.

The name Wilson also seems to be a great favourite with Watson, appearing in 'The Red-Headed League, 'The Dancing Men', 'The Golden Pince-Nez, as an aside in 'Black Peter' ("Wilson the notorious canary trainer") and four times for four different people in *The Valley of Fear.* Wilson Kemp is a character in 'The Greek Interpreter, and in *The Hound of the Baskervilles* the manager of 'one of the district messenger offices' smiles warmly at Holmes because, as Sherlock says, "Ah, Wilson, I see you have not forgotten the little case [not recorded by Watson] in which I had the good fortune to help you." In addition to all this, John (original James) Clay plays a prominent part in 'The Red-Headed League. But the penultimate name on the memorial stone, just above that of John Wilson, is JOHN WATSON.

So was the man Sherlock met in a laboratory at Bart's an impostor? Could he, even, have been a ward-orderly at Netley who learned enough to decide, when the opportunity unexpectedly arose, to pass himself off as a (not too competent) medical man? Remember 'Young

Stamford' hardly recognised him, and went so far as to ask what he had been doing with himself since they last met as he was "as thin as a lath and as brown as a nut"(*A Study in Scarlet*)? However, Watson obviously bore a superficial resemblance to a man Stamford was persuaded he knew and was willing to introduce to Sherlock Holmes. But how was it that the two older men never met in the chemistry laboratories at Bart's before, while Watson was supposedly in training there? Perhaps because he was, in reality, never anywhere near them until his spurious former dresser took him into the building. And here in the Minster was a ready-made history for him. Filling it out by writing about enteric fever, Portsmouth jetty, and the troopship *Orontes* was child's play to Watson if he had worked, or still did work, in The Royal Victoria Military Hospital at Netley; where he could pick up all kinds of useful information from men who *had* been at Maiwand.

All there was to do after that was borrow a sun-ray lamp to increase the tan (*A Study in Scarlet*) got when wheeling wounded officers round the grounds and, like them, keep his handkerchief up his sleeve (*The Crooked Man*). Then, hey presto, even the Great Detective was deceived. It's a sobering thought.

The above piece and the one proceeding it first appeared in The Baker Street Bugle and also The School Report.

HEDUNIT

Sagittarius is mentioned in the article about Beverley Minster. But who was she? Someone who wrote not only for the *London Mystery Magazine* (which asked for contributions to be sent to 'the best known private postal direction in the world', i.e. 221B Baker Street) but also for numerous other journals and newspapers, including the *New Statesman* and the *Daily Herald.*

Born in London in 1896, of Jewish parents who had fled from Russian pogroms, Olga Katzin-Miller married an actor and became an established writer on social, political and satirical verse before dying, at the age of ninety, in 1987. Here is what she wrote about Holmes:

Crime marches on, but detection is faster,
Nemesis silently pads behind;
Confident criminal come to disaster,
The game's afoot and the clues unwind;
Hot on the scent we follow the master,
Follow the master mind.

Holmes at the head of a lynx-eyed procession,
Holmes, with tight lips and countenance pale,
Holmes in the van of the sleuthing profession,
Holmes, stepping in where the Yard must fail.
Tecs and Inspectors in endless succession
Follow the Sherlock trail.

Follow the snake down the rope, through the transom,
Follow the hound to the Devonshire tor,
Follow the rubies, an Emperor's ransom,
Follow to India the Sign of the Four,
Follow the lead of the vanishing hansom
Starting from Sherlock's door.

The speed of the chase was not then supersonic,
 The pace of the cab-horse a steady clip-clop,
The cult of detection was still embryonic,
The joy of the man-hunt confined to the cop.
 Did he guess that he'd started, that wizard sardonic,
Something that would not stop?

Started a mania for singular cases,
Started a craving few addicts restrain,
Started a saga of amateur aces,
Whimsical, taciturn, dashing, urbane,
Started the public on hair-raising chases.
Study the scarlet stain!

Brains against brains of the underworld pitted, Tingling
excitement of fictional crime,
Mysteries solved, with loose ends neatly knitted,
Solved with a nonchalance more than sublime.
Millions of Watsons, supremely dim-witted,
Having a terrible time.

Bullet-hole, blow-pipe, mysterious injection,
Time-table, alibi, manor-house plan,
Fanciful flights in deductive detection
For highbrow and lowbrow and middlebrow fan;
But who does not turn, with a pang of affection,
Back where it all began?

Back from crime in the third dimension,
Back to problems more concrete,
Back to the well-spring of invention,
Back to the elementary feat.
Back to the cab, I need not mention,
Standing in Baker Street.

All still follow with Sherlock leading
Over the edge of time's abyss.
Wave a hand to those wheels receding,
Settle down to an hour of bliss.
But for Holmes you would not be reading,
Reading, dear reader, this.

A WRITER'S VIEW POINT

Roger (father of the noted Sherlockian Scholar, Richard) Lancelyn Green on *Alice in Wonderland*:
'More adults enjoy Lewis Carroll than any other children's author, though a select few – it may be MacDonald or Milne, Kipling or Tolkien, Lang or C. S. Lewis – are probably not as far behind as is commonly supposed, just as Rider Haggard and Conan Doyle retain their place securely among much greater novelists and story-tellers.'

A drawing from 'The Iron Pirate' by Max (*Wheels of Anarchy*) Pemberton, published in *Chums*, 1892.

Pemberton was the first editor of *Chums,* brought out as a rival to the *Boy's Own Paper.*

And one by Sidney Paget from 'Silver Blaze' by Arthur Conan (*The Memoirs of Sherlock Holmes*) Doyle, published in *The Strand Magazine,* December 1892:

'MY GOD, HOW THE TIME PASSES IN THIS PURSUIT!'

Jay Finley Christ, a Professor of Business Law at the University of Chicago for thirty years from 1920 to 1950, was one of the 'first generation' of American Sherlockian scholars. In 1946 an article by him appeared in the first issue of the 'Baker Street Journal', and he was invested into 'The Baker Street Irregulars' in 1949 as 'The Final Problem'.

Christ wrote regularly for the *Chicago Tribune,* signing himself 'Finch', and a collection of his pieces appeared in 1963 in a limited edition of 200 as *Finch's Final Fling.* He also wrote (1947) *An Irregular Chronology of Sherlock Holmes of Baker Street.* But perhaps his main claim to fame were the 'Christ codes', a form of shorthand which he used when referring to any or all of Sherlock's investigations – fifty-six short stories and four full-length tales – to save having to write the titles out in full every time he had to refer to or collate them. 'A Scandal in Bohemia' became SCAN, 'The Red-Headed League' REDL, 'A Case of Identity' IDEN, etc. Down to the final tale SHOS ('Shoscombe old Place') in which a newly dead body was hidden in an old coffin, once the original contents had been removed.

It will probably come as a surprise to the general reader that hundreds, if not thousands, of societies dedicated to the study of Sherlock Holmes exist all over the world. Christ himself founded a 'scion' society, 'The Hound of the Baskerville[s]', in Chicago. A scion society had to be approved first by that most prestigious American Sherlock Holmes Society of all, named after a group of ragamuffins Sherlock called upon to help him in *The Sign of Four* (a rip-roaring tale of bloody murder and stolen treasure), 'The Baker Street Irregulars'.

The man in charge of the B.S.I. is known as 'Wiggins' and, unlike the other Sherlockian societies, membership is by invitation only. Two American Presidents, Franklin D. Roosevelt and Harry S. Truman, were honorary members, and each person 'invested' takes something from the Canon as his title. For example, 'The Ancient British Barrow' or 'The Ill-Dressed Vagabond'.

'His' is used advisedly here. Up until 1991, no woman was permitted to be an Irregular (there were no girls in Sherlock's gang!) and this led to the formation of ASH: 'The Adventuresses of Sherlock Holmes', which meets in New York City and (before 1991) allowed a few men honorary membership, granting full membership to the opposite sex in 2008. For those not too familiar with the Sherlock Holmes stories, in Arthur Conan Doyle's first tale for the *Strand Magazine* ('A Scandal in Bohemia') the adventuress Irene Adler, former mistress of the King of Bohemia, lived in a house in Serpentine Mews - in that part of London known as St. John's Wood. So it's no surprise that The Adventuresses call their magazine 'The Serpentine Mews' and periodic collections of the best pieces published in it 'Serpentine Muse –ings'!

The following 'poem' by 'Jay Finlay Christ' [*sic*] is taken from *The Sherlock Holmes Scrapbook* edited by Peter Haining and published by the New English Library in 1973. Although it's all about Watson's "travel-worn and battered tin despatch-box" and its contents, the illustration which accompanies it is from 'The Musgrave Ritual'. Sherlock has opened his own "large box" - too heavy to carry - which he has pulled into their shared sitting room to reveal the investigations ("Not all successes, Watson") he conducted "before my biographer had come to glorify me."

In the vaults of Cox was an old tin box
With Watson's name on the lid.
What wouldn't we pay for that box today
And the secret notes there hid?

Old Russian dame, Ricoletti the lame,
The famous aluminium crutch;
For Alicia, the cutter, the parsley in butter,
What would you give for such?

Story of Randall, Darlington scandal,
The Coptic patriarchs,
The opal tiara, the Addleton barrow -
Dollars? Or francs? Or marks?

The tale of the pinch of Victor Lynch,
The furniture warehouse mob,
The case of the Hague, the murder in Prague,
The powder-less Margate job.

The giant rat, the cardinal's hat,
The Patersons (first name Grice),
The cormorant's bill, the Hammerford will -
We'd take 'em at *any* price.

The Phillimore fella who sought an umbrella,
The steamer Friesland (Dutch),
For Colonel Carruthers or Atkinson brothers
One never could give too much.

The Vatican case and its cameo face,

The slithering unknown worm,
The Abergavenny were none too many –
Where is this Cox's firm?

Oh, wonderful box in the vaults of Cox!
You come with a touch of salt!
But I offer two blocks of choicest stocks
For the treasure of Cox's vault.

FROM STUD TO SHOS

My thanks are due to the noted Sherlockian scholar, Karen Murdock, for sending me a copy of this poem by Gavin Brend which first appeared in 'The Sherlock Holmes Journal' vol.1, no. 2 (September 1952):

Our thanks are due to Dr. Christ
For giving us this helpful list.
It really gives me great relief
To think for once I can be brief.
I feel I could survive the loss
Of RETI, RESI, SUSS or SHOS,
But I intend to hold on fast
To 6NAP, REDH, BRUC and LAST;
Nor will I take the slightest chance
Of losing BERY, STOC or DANC.
You can have ILLU, 3GAR, BLAN,
But leave me DEVI, LADY, SCAN,
PRIO, EMPT, IDEN, NAVA, GLOR,

DYIN and LION, SPEC and NORW.
And now I have a batch for you –
NOBL and MAZA, CARD and CROO,
3STU and FINA, CHAS and CREE.
MISS is a case I'll never miss,
If you will leave me REIG and TWIS.
I'm far too mercenary to stop
My lust for GOLD and SILV and COPP.
I solemnly bequeath you THOR
And turn now to the longer four –
For you the STUD, for me the SIGN,
Yours is the VALL. The HOUN is mine.
I think it would be crazy folly
To rob you of REDC or SOLI,
But hope you will not misconstrue
My plea to leave me BLAC and BLUE!
Although in youth I liked it well,
To-day I'll let you have your YELL.
FIVE's yours, to that I will agree.
The other five belong to me*.
All thanks again, kind Doctor Christ,
For giving us this handy list.
*ABBE, ENGR, SECO, 3GAR and WIST

Sharp-eyed readers will notice the absence of BOSC, but Brend has been skilful enough to weave in the codes for all the other tales.

A 'SIGN' OF OUR TIMES?

Was Sherlock Holmes a religious man? The only time we hear of him being in church is when, disguised as "a drunken-looking groom" [SCAN], he's dragged in to witness the marriage of Irene Adler to Godfrey Norton. He does, however, occasionally come out with conventional expressions of a religious sort: Christmas is "the season of forgiveness" [BLUE], "What is the meaning of it, Watson? What object is served by this circle of misery and violence and fear? It must tend to some end, or else our universe is ruled by chance, which is unthinkable" [CARD] and, to the childless widow Mrs. Ronder [VEIL], "Your life is not your own. Keep your hands off it." In NAVA Holmes goes into raptures over a rose and says that the highest assurance of the goodness of Providence seems to him to rest in the flowers. And he knows his bible [CROO]. Nevertheless, it doesn't stop him from recommending a certain book to Watson which, if the Doctor hadn't been too much in love to read it [SIGN], might have given him pause. *The Martyrdom of Man* by Winwood Reade was, according to Sherlock, "one of the most remarkable ever penned."

A history of civilisation which moved away from the idea of a personal God towards an unthinkable impersonal force and finally to man alone, the book became a best-seller for the Victorians – asserting that not only would humans subdue the forces of evil without, they would also conquer those within themselves by subduing their own basic instincts (which the animal part of their nature has inherited from the lower beasts). Man would worship his own innate divinity, and find idleness and stupidity abhorrent. Women would become the companions (that is, the equals) of men, and the teachers of their children. As for science, it would eventually eradicate disease, inhibit decay and make immortality possible. "And then, the earth being small, mankind will emigrate into space." Through science, he ["perfect man"] will inhabit a body changed in ways not capable of understanding at the present time, master the forces of nature, become architects of systems and manufacturers of worlds, and "be what the vulgar worship as God."

It's easy to imagine how such a philosophy could grip the minds of men as confident of progress as the Victorians (even if the ultra-conservative Watson found the author's speculations too daring for his taste) and also to see how such ideas inform our present society, with its need to control the resources of the planet and its concentration on space travel!

Later in the investigation Holmes is discussing some workers coming out of a ship-yard by the Thames, calling them "Dirty looking rascals, but I suppose everyone has some little immortal spark concealed about them. You would not think it to look at them. There is no *a priori* probability about it. A strange enigma is man!" Once again Winwood Reade is brought into play. He "is good upon the subject" saying, according to Sherlock, that "While the individual man is an insoluble puzzle, in the aggregate he becomes a mathematical certainty. You can, for example, never foretell what any one man will do, but you can say with precision what an average number will be up to. Individuals vary, but the percentages remain constant. So says the statistician." But Watson has passed up the opportunity to study that gentleman and his atheistic tendencies. Someone, he can't quite remember who, describes man as "a soul concealed in an animal."

All the same, Reade remained extremely popular. So much so that Leonard Cottrell, as late as 1956, begins one of his own volumes with a long quotation from *The Martyrdom of Man*, calling it a "great work" and saying "There could be no better introduction to [my] book on Egypt." [*The Lost Pharaohs*, Pan Piper, p. 13]

SHERLOCK IN THE SPRING TIME

Although Holmes' investigations, as recorded by Watson, take place throughout the year, the period March through May appears to be the time when the detective was at his busiest.

There are occasions when the Doctor dates his accounts in relation to his marriage to Mary Morstan. However, he is so uncertain when the wedding took place that the reference is hardly helpful. At least one case is so sensitive that neither the year "nor even the decade" must be mentioned. He can, however, occasionally be very particular. In 'A Scandal in Bohemia' he calls on Holmes on the 20th of March, 1888. Otherwise investigations in this period occur in "the spring" or "in early spring." For example, 'The Speckled Band', 'The Solitary Cyclist', 'The Yellow Face' and 'The Copper Beeches'.

'A Scandal in Bohemia' introduces the woman who outwitted Holmes. In later pastiches by other writers she is sometimes presented as a love-interest for Sherlock. But Watson is adamant that Holmes called her 'the woman' and thought of her as such simply because she *did* get the better of him. 'The Speckled Band' sees the detective fighting off a deadly poisonous snake. In 'The Solitary Cyclist' a governess is rescued from an illegal marriage. 'The Yellow Face' is a story about racism and in 'The Copper Beeches' an innocent young woman is employed to take part in a cunning masquerade.

Other investigations in March, April or May are 'The Reigate Squire', in which Sherlock is nearly strangled, 'The Empty House' from where Moriarty's henchman, Colonel Sebastian Moran, is preparing to get Holmes with an air-rifle, 'The Priory School' (involving not only the kidnapping of the son of the Duke of Holdernesse but the unusual pocketing of a very large fee by our hero), the investigation into the goings-on in Wisteria Lodge and 'The Devil's Foot', a weird tale of wholesale slaughter which Holmes, by telegram, uncharacteristically suggests that Watson writes up saying, "Why not tell them of the Cornish horror – strangest case I ever handled."

It is just possible to include Miss Mary Sutherland's matrimonial misfortunes, caused by her disguised step-father, in this list ('A Case of Identity'). Or even an investigation which Watson simply labels "Early in 1896." And the last story of all ('Shoscombe Old Place'), where it is so vital for a man to win a horse-race before his creditors get to him that he hides his dead sister in a coffin in the family vault – first dislodging the original occupant and burning the bones in the family furnace. Watson tells the reader that it's May, the start of the flat-racing season.

But there can be no doubt when two of the most famous investigations – 'The Final Problem' and the book-length 'The Hound of the Baskervilles' – takes place. Internal evidence shows that the first was in April, and the second in May. As most people know who are not new to the Sherlock Holmes *Adventures,* 'The Final Problem' ends in a death struggle at the Reichenbach Falls, when Sherlock (to the disappointment of his many fans) supposedly goes to his death locked in mortal combat with his arch-enemy, Professor Moriarty. 'The Hound of the Baskervilles' re-introduced Holmes to his relieved readers after he was brought back from the dead by popular demand.

Anyone can be Sherlock at the Fatal Falls

DOYLE ON DOYLE (1)

Given the continuing compulsion to mine what by now can only be called the minutiae of Sherlockian (or should it be Holmesian? – the battle still rages) scholarship, perhaps it's time to consider what Conan Doyle himself said on the subject. In a letter written in 1893 to a New York journal called *The Critic,* after he had achieved world-wide fame and *anything* by him would probably sell well, he protested strongly against the unauthorised publication of his very early stories. They were meant, said Doyle, to have the ephemeral life they deserved and "it is slightly annoying to an author when work which he has deliberately suppressed is resuscitated against his will."[1]

However, the main thrust of his letters to the press shows a robust common sense, curiosity and, on the whole, a fair amount of liberal-mindedness. How foolish to let loose a detachment of diseased prostitutes on soldiers returning to Portsmouth Harbour after service in India because the suspension of the Contagious Diseases Act prevents doctors from offending the women's modesty by giving them medical examinations. How idiotic to give any publicity to someone who objected to members of the Young Men's Christian Association [the Y.M.C.A.] singing 'worldly songs' in church: "What, because Mr. Young is Vicar of St. John's shall there be no more cakes and ale in the land?" What right had W. H. Smith to exclude George Moore's controversial novel *Esther Waters* from its railway station bookstalls? It was the duty of a distributor to distribute, not act as an unofficial censor.

Nothing if not practical, Doyle wanted to see cavalry replaced by bicycles in the interests of speed and efficiency, as well as expense. But he would never believe the change had taken place "until I see 100 lightly equipped men, with rifles slung on their backs, and bandoliers across their chests, riding behind the King's State Carriage in place of the present picturesque but medieval guard."

Many of Doyle's later letters deal with the more outré aspects of spiritualism, as well as his firm belief in the existence of fairies. But it's pleasant to discover that his very last letter, printed in the *Daily Telegraph* on the day he died, is a perfectly lucid comment on the disastrous expedition to the Dardenelles during WW1.

[1] See 'The Listener' 27/2/1986 p. 23

DOYLE ON DOYLE (2)

Conan Doyle once described to one of London's 'bright young things' [1] how he set about writing a detective story about Holmes and Watson, giving as an example *The Speckled Band.*

Since he said he could no more sit down and command ideas than he could sit down and command rain, he had to wait for an idea suddenly, and for no apparent reason, to come to him. When the inspiration for this particular tale arrived, it turned out to be about a man killing somebody with a snake in order to benefit from a will. "I thought the idea a good one, and thinking of it made it gradually grow. So, after very little thought, I had an unscrupulous man planning to murder his stepdaughter."

Doyle decided to make the murderer a man who had lived in India. Would he, therefore, know more than most men about poisonous snakes? Did he have a collection of books on snakes? Having chosen his characters, all that remained for the author to do was to "concoct false scents to keep the reader guessing to the end, and pick out from dozens of possibilities clues for the detective to follow up." Although these had to be "as ingenious as possible, the difficulty is not in imagining them, but in selecting them."

But Holmes "wasn't really *big* enough. The other day I wrote a whole Sherlock Holmes story, and finished it, and played two rounds of golf on the same day. Now, if you take Professor Challenger, that's a different story."

[1]Beverley Nichols in *Are They the Same at Home*? First published by John Murray in 1935

A REGIMENT ON WHEELS

This idea originated in Europe during the nineteenth century when Germany and Austria (as well as France) employed military personnel as armed despatch riders, who could also act as a means of defence. During the siege of Paris they supplemented the so-called 'balloon post' and later, further afield, when a South African town was being attacked by the Boers, Cape of Good Hope stamps (bearing pictures of 'Hope Sitting' and 'Hope Standing') were surcharged by the beleaguered garrison "Mafeking Besieged" and used on letters carried through enemy territory by intrepid cyclists telling the outside world what had happened. When the supply of these particular stamps ran out, a local stamp was printed showing an orderly on his bicycle – again bearing the surcharge MAFEKING BESIEGED.

Britain aimed to recruit 20,000 volunteer cyclists to join the army: and it wasn't long before each battalion had a detachment of riders on its pay-roll. One of the first set of 'bike riders' was the 26th Middlesex which, by 1888, had its own Head-Quarters in Queen Street, Chelsea, opposite the famous 'hospital' for retired soldiers. Very well equipped and comfortable, the men kept their bicycles in the stables, which were open at the front for a quick getaway, and the main building housed a sergeant's mess, a lecture hall, a canteen and a smoking-room for officers, whose living quarters were hung with pictures. These paintings included 'The Last Eleven at Maiwand' which definitely resonates with Conan Doyle and his creation of Watson, wounded in that battle and sent home just in time to meet Holmes.

Dismounting to defend a Road Late in the 19th century

THE DOLL AND ITS MAKER

The following example of doggerel verse, by Arthur Guiterman (1871-1943), appeared in the American magazine 'Life' in 1912 and, shortly afterwards, 'London Opinion.' The American spelling has been retained, and it can be seen that the writer has had to struggle for some of his rhymes. Famous for his humour, he published thousands of pieces of light verse in newspapers, magazines and book-length collections, co-founded the Poetry Society of America and became its President in 1925. Guiterman also founded 'The Woman's Home Companion' and the 'Literary Digest', both of which also published much of his verse. Verse which, while retaining its funny side, often had a philosophic bent:

> Now motor roads are dustless,
> The latest steel is rustless,
> Our tennis courts are sodless,
> Our new religions, godless

Rust is mentioned again in another amusing piece, 'On the Vanity of Earthly Greatness':

> The tusks which clashed in mighty brawls
> Of mastodons are billiard balls.

> The sword of Charlemagne the Just
> Is Ferric Oxide, known as rust.

> The grizzly bear, whose potent hug
> Was feared by all, is now a rug.

Great Caesar's bust is on the shelf,
And I don't feel so well myself.

Born in Vienna of American parents, his attack on Conan Doyle, while appearing gentlemanly, nevertheless contains several barbs. The British author has been 'prodigiously lucky' and it's difficult to see how he came by 'so splendid a revenue'. He steals plots and methods of writing without any acknowledgement. Reading this, one can't avoid the implication that his work (containing 'Plenty that's slovenly') was not worth the fees it commanded.

As to 'England's South African raid', this attracted world-wide condemnation and, according to Guiterman, Conan Doyle (who spent three months as a volunteer doctor in a Bloemfontein hospital) had sought to justify it in a short pamphlet ('volume'): 'The War in South Africa: Its Cause and Its Course and Conduct.' The American, needing a rhyme for 'vindicates' introduces the mysterious Syndicate, a partnership between Cecil Rhodes (who owned the de Beer Diamond Mine in South Africa) and a London-based cartel of diamond merchants who kept the price of diamonds artificially high. If the Boers had not been defeated things might have gone badly for them and their business.

Although Doyle had received his knighthood from King Edward VII by the time Guiterman came to write about his career, the "cross with a chain to it" was simply an honour and involved no precedence of any kind. This 'Order of St. John', abolished at the Reformation, was re-instated in Britain in 1888, the gift of the Sovereign for those who had worked in hospitals.

We discover towards the end of the diatribe that the writer prefers 'adventures and fierce dinotheriums' rather than 'Hewlett's ecstatic deliriums.' 'Dinotheriums' is obviously a reference to the 'terrible wild beasts' in Conan

Doyle's first Professor Challenger novel *The Lost World* published in 1912. And Maurice Henry Hewlett (1861-1926), although not much read today, was a prolific British writer with an enormous following. He wrote historical romances and in 1912, the year that most concerns us here, published *Helen Redeemed and Other Poems* - the dedication alone perhaps justifying Guiterman's opinion of his work.

Be that as it may, the American seems to be a long way from having an unqualified admiration for Doyle's writing; and one can only admire the courteousness of the latter's reply, which appeared in 'London Opinion' later that year. It certainly reads more spontaneously, and is (mercifully) considerably shorter. But first, Arthur Guiterman:

TO SIR ARTHUR CONAN DOYLE

Gentle Sir Conan, I'll venture that few have been
Half as prodigiously lucky as you have been.
Fortune, the flirt! has been wondrously kind to you.
Ever beneficent, sweet and refined to you.

Doomed though you seemed, one might swear without perjury,
Doomed to the practise of physic and surgery,
Yet, growing weary of pills and physicianing,
Off to the Arctic you packed, expeditioning.

Roving and dreaming, Ambition, that heady sin,
Gave you a spirit too restless for medicine.
That, I presume, as Romance is the quest of us,

Made you an Author –the same as the rest of us.

"Ah," but the rest of us clamour distressfully,
"How do you manage the game so successfully?
Tell us, disclose to us how under Heaven you
Squeeze from the inkpot so splendid a revenue!"

Then, when you published your volume that vindicates
England's South African raid (or the Syndicate's),
Pleading that England's extreme bellicosity
Wasn't (as most of us think) an atrocity,

Straightway they gave you a cross with a chain to it – (oh,
what an honor! I could not attain to it,
Not if I lived to the age of Methusalem!)
Made you a Knight of St. John of Jerusalem!

Faith, as a teller of tales you've the trick with you!
Still there's a bone I've been wanting to pick with you:
Holmes is your hero of drama and serial:
All of us know where you dug the material!

Whence he was moulded – 'tis almost a platitude;
Yet your detective, in shameless ingratitude –
Sherlock your sleuth-hound with motives ulterior
Sneers at Poe's Dupin as "very inferior!"

Labels Gaboriau's clever Lecoq, indeed,
Merely "a bungler," a creature to mock, indeed!
This, when your plots and your methods in story owe
More than a trifle to Poe and Gaboriau.

Sets all the Muses of Helicon sorrowing.
Borrow, Sir Knight, but be decent in borrowing!
Still let us own that your bent is a cheery one,
Little you've written to bore or to weary one.

Plenty that's slovenly, nothing with harm in it,
Much with abundance of vigor and charm in it.
Give me detectives with brains analytical
Rather than weaklings with morals mephitical –

Stories of battles and man's intrepidity
Rather than wails of neurotic morbidity!
Give me adventures and fierce dinotheriums
Rather than Hewlett's ecstatic deliriums!

Frankly, Sir Conan, some hours I've eased with you
And, on the whole, I am pretty well pleased with you.

AND SIR ARTHUR'S REPLY

Sure there are times when one cries with acidity,
'Where are the limits of human stupidity?'
Here is a critic who says as a platitude
That I am guilty because 'in ingratitude
Sherlock, the sleuth-hound, with motives ulterior,
Sneers at Poe's Dupin as 'very inferior.'
Have you not learned, my esteemed commentator,
That the created is not the creator?
As the creator I've praised to satiety

Poe's Monsieur Dupin, his skill and variety,
And have admitted that in my detective work
I owe to my model a deal of selective work.
But is it not on the verge of inanity
To put down to me my creation's crude vanity?
He, the created, would scoff and would sneer,
Where I, the creator, would bow and revere.
So please grip this fact with your cerebral tentacle:
The doll and its maker are never identical.

SHERLOCK IN THE FORBIDDEN CITY

Readers of *The Strand Magazine* in 1903-4 were delighted to discover that Holmes had not after all gone to his death at the Reichenbach Falls. But, although Moriarty was dead, two of the most dangerous members of his gang were still at large: and they just happened to be, as Sherlock said, "my own most vindictive enemies."

So, instead of returning to London, he "travelled for two years in Tibet." Where he "amused" himself "by visiting Lhassa and spending some days with the head Llama." Holmes "then passed through Persia, looked in at Mecca, and paid a short but interesting visit to the Khalifa at Khartoum."

This was not done, of course, in the detective's own name. As he said to Watson, "You may have read of the remarkable explorations of a Norwegian named Sigerson, but I am sure that it never occurred to you that you were receiving news of your friend."

Conan Doyle may also have read about the remarkable exploits of a certain explorer. One who, in 1897, published a book about his travels in Persia. As well as this, Sven Anders Hedin, born in Stockholm in 1865, wrote accounts of his extensive explorations of Tibet; and in 1901 described his unsuccessful attempts to visit the 'Forbidden City' of Lhasa – at that time closed to Europeans.

So do we have here an example of an author making good use of something already in the public domain? If so, it isn't necessarily a bad thing. Establishing a resonance ("Now, where have I heard/read this before?") increases most readers' interest in a writer's work, making them eager for more of the same; and in this instance Conan Doyle seems to have gone one better by allowing his most famous creation to visit the Capital of Tibet in spite of the prohibition; almost (from the sound of it) by invitation. A feat we may have come to expect from the omnipotent Holmes, but somewhat marred by Watson's faulty spelling!

There are minor changes. Sigerson is Norwegian, not Swedish, even though Norway didn't become officially independent until a year after 'The Adventure of the Empty House' was first published in *The Strand*. And Sven Hedin is almost exclusively associated with explorations in Asia, with no excursions to the South of France. But presumably Sherlock Holmes abandoned his Sigerson disguise before beginning his researches into coal-tar derivatives at a laboratory in Montpelier.

FENIMORE COOPER (1789-1851)

"It's not a job up everybody's street. You have to be like one of those Red Indians I read about when I was a child, the fellows who never let a twig snap beneath their feet." *Aunts Aren't Gentlemen* by P. G. Wodehouse.

The American James Fenimore Cooper wrote a series of books called *Leather Stocking Tales.* These included *The Last of the Mohicans,* an exciting story perfect for the young, about an Indian tracker famous for being able to move silently through the forest on moccasin-clad feet. However, as well as being familiar with Red-Indian territory, Cooper spent many years travelling and writing in Europe. Here is what he said in his book *Recollections of Europe* about his visit to some famous Falls.

"The stream, a clear brawling, sparkling brook of the largest class, tumbles suddenly off the last pitch of the mountain (that on which we stood) into the valley. It is called the Reichenbach or the Rich Fall. A name it well deserves, the volume of its water, and its varied aspects, rendering it one of the richest cascades, to use the German term, I remember to have seen."

Which brings us to the vexed question of 'Fall' or 'Falls'? Non-Americans are inclined to put all falls into the plural. But American usage is more consistent. Niagara has two 'falls' the Reichenbach one. But the editor of *The Strand Magazine* was also inconsistent. Watson writes, in 'The Final Problem', "We had strict instructions...on no account to pass the falls of Reichenbach." Later he says, on reaching the spot, "The path had been cut half-way round the fall to afford a compete view." From then on until the end of the tale he refers always to 'the fall' rather than 'the falls': "It took me more than two hours to get back to the fall." To find "the cry of the fall borne back to my ears," etc.

However, one of the drawings by Sidney Paget for 'The Final Problem' shows water coming from the glacier into a hanging valley and splitting into a number of small falls, before debouching into a chasm to form a huge body of water. One which is all that can be seen from the platform opposite the narrow path where Holmes stood pensively awaiting his fate. A spot now marked by a large white cross high up on the black, slippery cliff-wall behind. And here is what Cooper wrote about Netley Abbey nearly forty years before Watson began his training to be an army doctor in the area and had the chance to see it if he wished. According to the American, the ruin was a fine, without being an imposing, building - with a particular window the finest part. If he could have seen it under construction and then as a working abbey his "thoughts would have been very different from those of the graveyard." But it was easy in its present state to "people its passages with Benedictines stalking along its galleries and fancy the choir pealing among its arches."

A number of London cockneys arrived and, after lighting a fire on the grass surrounding the Abbey, were trying to organise a brew-up. Cooper speculated (before leaving in a hurry) that the invite must have been "to tea and ruins."

The Reverend R. H. Barham, author of *The Ingoldsby Legends,* also had thoughts of the monks patrolling the Abbey in those far-off days:

Then came the Abbot, with mitre and ring,
With pastoral staff and all that sort of thing,
And a Monk with a book, and a Monk with a bell,
And 'dear little souls',
In clean linen stoles,
Swinging their censers, and making a smell –
And see where the Choir-master walks in the rear,
With front severe,
And brow austere,
Now and then pinching a little boy's ear
When he chants the responses too late or too soon, Or his
Do, Re, Mi, Fa, So, La's not quite in tune.

He then goes on to tell the reader, rather unpleasantly, that a nun was walled up in the Abbey for winking at a gardener's boy, and says there was talk (towards the middle of the eighteenth century) of a woman's skeleton being found in a cellar there.

The Ruins of Netley Abbey

THE ORIGINS OF TREE WORSHIP

In 'The Empty House' Sherlock Holmes comes back from the dead disguised as an elderly deformed man and carrying a number of books. Watson inadvertently causes him to drop these and, picking them up, sees one on the origin of tree worshp.

The Doctor regards this as an "obscure volume." But dates are important here. Doyle began writing for *The Strand Magazine* in 1891, the year after the first two volumes of Frazer's *The Golden Bough* were published. Although the murder of Ronald Adair is set in 1894, the story of the Empty House didn't appear in *The Strand Magazine* until October, 1901, very shortly after Frazer published his third volume.[1] That author's thesis was that tree worship had developed from very early times and was perfectly natural - since the earth then was so covered by forests that "the scattered clearings must have appeared like islets in an ocean of green."

Trees were thought to have senses. They could feel pain. Frazer recounts a horrific story of a man who had his navel cut out for harming a tree and was forced to run round it until his "guts" had fully encircled the trunk to compensate for the wanton damage to its bark. A 'sacred' tree stood at the entrance to each primitive village and was worshipped by the villagers, the souls of whose ancestors were said to have migrated to it when they died. There were instances of trees being planted on graves so that their vitality could prevent the corruption of the corpse buried beneath. As late as the nineteenth century woodmen in parts of Austria and Germany apologised formally to a tree (in order to avoid ill-luck) before cutting it down. So maybe the 'bookseller's' volume wasn't so obscure after all.

[1] He went on to publish 12 more volumes between 1911 and 1915

SHALL WE JOIN THE LADIES?

Fictional female detectives in the nineteenth and early twentieth century had to have a very pressing reason for entering what was mainly a male preserve. Loveday Brooke, for example, was desperately poor. And as late as 1898 Dorcas Deane ("A real sob-sister was Dorcas") worked to support an artist husband who had gone blind. Even so, some women still didn't escape becoming social outcasts, which is probably why the gloriously named Miss van Snoop made only one appearance. Florence Cusack, however, was an exception. Young, beautiful and wealthy, she travelled from country to country trying to clear her dead husband's name in a series of stories and (most unusually) "ended up in the arms of her narrator."

Madelyn Mack, "the delightful, golden-haired and beautiful college girl" invented by the American writer Hugh C. Weir, had to earn her own living and decided to copy Sherlock Holmes, referring to her "dissecting-room experiences" and using expressions which do credit to him as a model. She was also fond of staging dramatic denouments. But her admiration for the man wasn't unqualified, and she later became rather dismissive of him. There were, said Miss Mack, only two rules in detection: hard work and common sense. "Not uncommon sense, like our friend Sherlock Holmes."

However, like Sherlock, Miss Mack had "a grip of steel" and was not averse to drug-taking, although the coca berry was her stimulant rather than cocaine. She also had her 'Watson'. Miss Noraker ('Nora') was on hand to ask questions, and to say things like "I'm afraid I don't quite follow you. There is nothing at all out of the ordinary that I can catch." And, like John H. Watson, she doesn't always know where Madelyn is or what she's up to. Nevertheless, Nora too is prepared to go anywhere with little or no notice, and at any time of the day or night. Her reference to "the tyrant of our city editor's desk" implies that she also wrote up Madelyn's investigations in the best Watsonian manner.

Then there is the little helper of "Lady Molly of Scotland Yard." Unlike Miss Noraker, Baroness Orczy's 'Mary' appears to be a servant of some sort, and has the very irritating habit of referring to her employer as "my dear lady" at the end of every sentence. She sounds even more admiring than *the* Watson.

But the road was being well-paved for today's feisty forensic females.

LET'S HEAR IT FOR BOHEMIA

"The rough-and-tumble of Afghanistan, coming on the top of a natural Bohemianism of disposition, has made me rather more lax than befits a medical man"- Watson in 'The Musgrave Ritual'.

"It was not a collection of residential flats, but rather the abode of Bohemian bachelors" - Watson again, in 'The Three Garridebs.'

As Holmes went out to pursue the elusive Mrs. Sawyer, Watson passed the time "skipping over the pages of Henri Murger's Vie de Boheme." A Study in Scarlet.

Murger's sketches of the true bohemian life, which he had lived himself, enjoyed enormous success as a series of newspaper articles. These later came out in book form, as a play and finally, half a century later, an opera by Puccini. Talented young artists, writers and sculptors with no money hung out in a derelict farm-house near the Barriere d'Enfer (one of the gates of Paris) coming regularly into the City hoping to earn the price of a cup of coffee at the Café Momus.

Murger, however, later became respectable, deserting the Momus for the Café Riche but continuing to write novels which painted the really bohemian existence in the grimest of colours. It led, he said, to The Academy, the Hospital, or the Morgue. There was nothing for it but extremely hard work, and young men without talent who simply wanted to sample the life did so knowing they could return home after a short, romantic and not too painfully poor stay in a garret, drinking in noisy taverns with genuine artists and sleeping with little grisettes.

As soon as the game palled they could go home, as Murger put it, "to marry their cousins and set up as solicitors in a town of thirty thousand souls where, sitting by the fire in the evening, they boasted of their poverty-stricken artist days with all the exaggeration of travellers describing a tiger-hunt."

A NOTEWORTHY ANNIVERSARY

In 1987 the Radio Times for December 5-11 printed a series of articles in honour of the first appearance a hundred years earlier of A Study Scarlet in Beeton's Christmas Annual.

Tim Piggott-Smith, one of the few actors to have played both Holmes and Watson, had this to say about the latter: "You always have to take [him] seriously as a practising doctor, and some of the bits that work best are when Watson is examining a victim and naming the bones which have been damaged." While this is a moot point for some of us and may have been made in stage productions rather than stressed in the canon, the Doctor "represents the average reader". He is there "so that Holmes can think out loud."

But, for Piggott-Smith, the most important point about Watson is that he stands for decency and straightness - the perfect upright citizen. And "It all serves to throw the character of Sherlock Holmes into even sharper relief." He, unlike the Doctor, is a strange man, with something chilling about him, a sense of cruelty beneath the surface. "If you had to choose between Holmes and Watson as holiday companions, you might find Watson a little dull, but a much easier person to be with [and] I think it's pretty terrific what Conan Doyle has achieved with him."

FINGERPRINTING

In 'The Norwood Builder', Inspector Lestrade draws Holmes' attention to what looks like a blood stain on a whitewashed wall and says, "You are aware that no two thumb marks are alike?"

Holmes says he has heard something of that kind, a remark made more meaningful if the reader knows that Edward Henry published a monograph, *Classification and Uses of Fingerprints* in the same year that this particular 'Adventure' appeared in *The Strand Magazine*.

Hundreds of years earlier Chinese potters were known to 'sign' their work with an individual thumb mark in the wet clay. But the earliest mention in the West of prints as a means of identification seems to have been in a paper read to The Royal Society by Neheramiah Grew in 1684, in which he mentions ridge patterns on the human finger.

A much later exponent of this phenomenon was Sir William Herschel. An official of the old East India Company, he was a magistrate in that part of India known then as East Bengal. As early as 1858 Herschel was insisting on a hand print, as well as a written application, from natives tendering for road-work; but the nearest he got to using fingerprints in criminal cases was to prevent the hiring of substitutes to serve jail sentences.

It was Francis Galton who suggested a register of fingerprints as a means of identifying, and thus more easily catching, criminals; and he published several papers, together with a book on the subject in 1893. Two years before, Edward Henry had had some correspondence with Galton and he later, in the manner of Sherlock Holmes, wrote the monograph already mentioned and which was published by the Government of India while Henry was working there for the British Raj.

In 1900 Henry was seconded to South Africa to organise the Civil Police in Pretoria and Johannesburg. The following year he was recalled to Britain, where he became Assistant Commissioner (Crime) in charge of the CID at Scotland Yard, and later Commissioner. He established the Metropolitan Police Fingerprint Bureau in 1901 and is widely regarded as one the great Commissioners, credited with "dragging the Metropolitan Police into the modern day and away from the class-ridden Victorian era." Fingerprinting was here to stay and, although it was initially used not to identify criminals but in some way to prevent habitual offenders from concealing their previous offences, effectively ousted Bertillon's less effectual method of measuring body parts.

WORK IN PROGRESS

"I suppose you've heard all about Miss Violet de Merville," I said to Emily one morning as we sat chatting in the garden of her house in Bayswater.

"The woman Sherlock Holmes, the man you admire so much, called 'The illustrious Client'?" she asked abstractedly, feigning indifference.

"And I might term 'The Noble Spinster', although that wouldn't really fit the case – since the man commonly supposed to be her father is only an old soldier who fought in Afghanistan."

"Just like another gentleman of our acquaintance," she said with a smirk. "Only he didn't."

"That's enough about Watson," I retorted angrily, leaning back in my chair and regarding her malevolently from under half-closed eyelids.

"She, this Miss de Merville, reminds me in some ways of another snob who added 'de' to his name. The man who styled himself James Hamilton Oscar de Wilde," said my dear colleague.

"James Wilder, the illegitimate son of the Duke of Holdernesse?   Well, it's more than likely she's illegitimate too."

"There have been rumours I know," said Emily blithely. "But nothing like those attached to the so-called Oscar."

"I've been told that if she'd been born on the right side of the blanket she might some day have become Queen of England!" said I, tapping my foot impatiently.

Emily gave me a startled look. "You're not telling me the King is her father?"

"Well, that would make the client illustrious enough to please even Sherlock Holmes – but, daughter or not, *she* was by no means the client I can tell you. However, since she showed the door to everyone who tried to rescue her from a most disastrous, not to say potentially fatal, marriage or, rather, ticked off a brow-beaten servant to do it, somebody important had to intervene."

As I said earlier, we were sitting in the garden of the house in Bayswater. Miss Fanshaw, as she sometimes called herself, had recently taken up painting. Long-handled brushes of various sizes were scattered about, and she held her palette at an angle as if she were Angelica Kaufmann herself – only a little more elegant. She had done a preliminary drawing of her old house in Lee, the one she and her husband left after he had to stop begging. But when I asked if her drawing was taken from memory she said no. She'd gone down to Kent and looked through the iron railings surrounding the property. The gardens, once described by the house agent as 'well laid out grounds', were sadly neglected, a circumstance which had given her quite a turn.

"Everything had gone to rack and ruin. That's what comes of having to get rid of a house in a hurry. One can't pick and choose the buyer. Neither can one hold out for the highest price. But when Mr Holmes and his dear friend warned Neville off begging…"

"Emily," I said, "it's true Watson was also included in the affair. Which allows you to get at me, even though John wasn't the one to warn Mr. St. Clair off. But it's years since your husband posed as the mendicant Hugh .Boone. Don't you think it's time to call a truce?"

She intended the painting to be for her dear daughter Grizelda's wedding in three week's time. Her son Freddy was already married, and my son Nipper had grown to be nearly as tall as his father. They often went fishing together, and The Nip was busy trying to decide whether to join the army as soon as he left school or go to university.

"But," said John, "there's plenty of time to decide on that sort of thing. Best enjoy the years you've still to go before thinking about Sandhurst or Bart's. As it happens Professor James Moriarty, after he lost his Chair of Mathematics at what Holmes termed 'one of our smaller universities' (a Chair he obtained on the strength of his work on asteroids at the very early age of twenty-one, mark you) was forced to coach candidates who were ambitious to get into the Military Academy. He didn't like doing it. Called the young men dunderheads."

"Thank goodness he's no longer around to coach Nip," I said, "or the boy might learn other things besides how to obtain a Commission in His Britannic Majesty's Forces. Coaching boys to pass the Entrance Exam into Sandhurst was one of Moriarty's 'respectable' jobs. It certainly never brought him in enough money to buy that Greuze."

"The girl 'keeking at you sideways', as Mr. Mac remarked when Holmes asked if he had seen the painting in the Napoleon of Crime's study?" said Watson. "Mr. MacDonald is a Police Inspector, my dear Nip; and it was Sherlock Holmes who gave Moriarty the nickname."

Now I sat looking at Mrs. St. Clair as she dabbed away at the canvas, more conscious of her appearance than she was of anything else. She often affected a little lace cap to cover a grey hair or two. That is, when she wasn't prancing around in waistcoat and trousers and wearing an altogether different type of headgear. An outfit she swore she only put on in the interests of The Watson-Fanshaw Detective Agency, but which was all the more galling because of the way she had kept her figure over the years.

After studying her painting with a critical eye for a few minutes, Emily suddenly reminded me of Miss de Merville. What was it I was supposed to have heard?

"She's upped and married the Duke of Loamshire, poor devil."

"What, with that family history? And her so particular!"

"Blinded by love, as usual. But the young man is very handsome. And I for one haven't heard anything against him, at least not since I wrote something about that investigation."

"Except that his aunt was hanged for murder!"

"I already knew that, and so did you. And I must say, murder seems to follow the girl around. She only just escaped the attentions of that Austrian killer, Baron Gruner."

"With whom we have had a great deal to do," said

Miss Fanshaw maliciously, "when he testified against your husband in court and helped to convict him of fraud." "

"This is all very interesting. But what I would like to know is, have you any idea where something for the Agency is going to come from?"

"Of course I have," she said. "I had a telephone call this morning; and what a lucky chance you came to see me."

"To go over old sores and watch you painting," I said, "instead of learning immediately that we had work to do. What is it we're about to investigate, if you would be so kind as to tell me at last?"

"I haven't the foggiest idea," said the infuriating woman, gathering up her easel and other artists' paraphernalia, "until I go back in the house and re-read the note on the telephone table."

"Watch out as you do go," I said. "It would be a shame to smudge that beautiful picture." This made me laugh so much I had to cough hurriedly into my handkerchief.

"You've paint on your nose," said Mrs. St. Clair coolly, "from coming too close to it."

She and I had had an uneasy friendship ever since our first meeting in Exeter Hall. One of Moriarty's agents, M. Poirot (the father of the twins Achille and Hercule), had given me instructions to collect a stick of dynamite from the place, put it in my bustle and march through London with a lot of other like-minded women to blow up the Houses of Parliament and other important buildings. 'Emily Fanshaw' wasn't involved. She had wandered in to see what was going on. We ended by leaving the Hall together. I threw my stick of dynamite into the river Thames and went home with her. She told me one of her aims in life was to find Jack the Ripper and asked if I would like to help. It ended with us going down to Whitechapel and nearly being murdered by Leather Apron. It also led to our forming the Watson-Fanshaw Detective Agency. We had many adventures after that, and some successes. Enough for us to be still working all these years later. Her husband, Neville, kept in the dark at first, helped us occasionally. But it was my husband John H. Watson's long association with Sherlock Holmes which gave us the advantage over other detective agencies. On both sides of the Atlantic.

As soon as we got into the house, and Emily had deposited her precious materials in the lobby, she went to the telephone table, picked up the note she had made and said, "I'll bet a pound to a pinch of salt that you will never guess who this is from."

"The Giant Rat of Sumatra," I said. "Or even The Hound of the Baskervilles."

"You're much too old for that kind of childish nonsense. It's from Sherlock Holmes himself."

"You have definitely made my day," I said sarcastically.

"Your personal animosities," said Emily primly, "ought to be set aside in the interests of the Watson-Fanshaw Detective Agency if you want to continue to build on our successes. I'm surprised at such lack of control."

This was rich, coming from such an impatient female.

"Mr. Holmes says Moriarty has left Sussex, taking a valuable set of house breaking tools with him – as well as every single one of the tobacco pipes."

"What, even the cherrywood? That will put a dent in the Great Detective's image."

"The jemmies, the pick-locks and all those monographs, which he hopes eventually to be able to use for his own purposes."

"Don't tell me Moriarty is going in for publishing his Memoirs," I said bitterly. "The world will soon be awash with writings about him and Sherlock bally Holmes. As well as all those others who were said to visit Baker Street."

"Which I am quite sure you, as an author, will thoroughly enjoy reading."

'And stealing for your own purposes' is what she would have liked to have said, I thought to myself – recalling my account of how Holmes went off with Moriarty at the end of *A Study in Crimson*. The idea being that the two men would set up house together on the Sussex Downs, with Holmes' old housekeeper, Mrs. Hudson, to look after them. What had John said as we stared out of the window at 'The Laurels' and watched them go? "I give it six months." How right he had been!

Aloud I asked, "Is it possible we can get back to Holmes' communication? That is, if he has anything of interest to impart besides his domestic troubles. Something which would be of use to a couple of working women."

"The telephone message is about Sir James Damery," said Emily.

"Don't tell me Baron Gruner has broken out again. The state he is in it should be next door to impossible."

"It's something concerning a will. Mr. Holmes says he has become so interested in his bees, and is now so fond of swimming, he can't be bothered with the case and would like to pass it on to us."

"I know what that means," I said. "We'll do all the donkey work and then he'll suddenly turn up to tell us where we went wrong. One member of the family has had more than enough of that. I aim to make sure he doesn't catch both of us."

"Well I have Grizelda's wedding to see to, so I suggest we consider the matter later. Meanwhile, I shall write to Mr. Holmes at his address on the Downs and say things will have to be kept on hold for a couple of weeks."

"For goodness sake don't tell him about the wedding. We can't have him turning up in Hanover Square. Unless of course you don't object to someone disguised as 'a simple minded clergyman' trying to officiate at the ceremony."

The crowd outside St. George's was quite large, and more than a little scruffy since many people from the poorer parts of London often turned out to see a society wedding. It was difficult to imagine why, but I always supposed it gave them a vicarious kind of enjoyment, perhaps just enough to brighten up their truly dreadful lives for a while. I couldn't help wondering to myself if some of Mr. St. Clair's acquaintances from his days as a beggar were there. If so, they wouldn't recognise him in his morning-dress and shiny top hat, along with his new boots and fashionable spats.

The young girl on his arm looked suitably modest behind her veil but swept into the church without any of the usual signs of nerves. She had inherited her mother's figure, and looked a stunner in her ivory wedding-dress. I was pleased to see from my seat near the altar that the Nipper was playing his part very creditably too as one of the ushers, with Freddy St. Clair as Chief Usher to keep them all in order.

I knew Watson, standing stiffly to attention as the bride came up the aisle with her father, would have loved to be in uniform. Nevertheless, he looked very well in *his* dress clothes, and I felt both my men were a great credit to me. The bride's mother had sent to Paris for a new parasol to match a very elegant outfit, and I also managed to turn myself out in quite a respectable way in my favourite colours of green and gold.

Just before the service started I had gone to examine the wedding presents set out on trestles in the hotel rooms Neville St. Clair had booked for what Emily said would be 'the reception of the year', to say nothing of the wedding. There were a great many gifts; and I saw two very well turned out gentlemen looking askance at the silver. Affecting nonchalance, I strolled over to where they stood and was not surprised to hear a familiar voice say smoothly, "Are you here in your public or private capacity?"

"Both," I said. "So keep your hands off those spoons." A. J. Raffles, pretending his interest was entirely aesthetic and that he had no notion what the monetary value of anything in the place could possibly be.

"I'm the bridegroom's uncle," he said, "and as such perfectly entitled to inspect the wedding presents."

"And I suppose your friend here is his brother?"

"Certainly not," said Bunny disdainfully. "The Manders Family…"

"Stow it, my Rabbit," said Raffles. "She's going to keep her beady eye on us whatever you say."

Uncle or not, I couldn't see either Raffles or Bunny being in church and felt sure that, if I hadn't been around, several of the wedding presents would have found their way to the nearest pawnshop. As might Mrs. St. Clair's painting of the house at Lee. This was much admired, and brought tears to the eyes of some people who wished they were still living there. I only hoped we would escape the usual remarks from Emily about Holmes and the way he warned her husband off mendicancy. When, according to her, Neville St. Clair was all but ruined.

Things had certainly picked up at 'The Laurels' since then, however. Or how could they have afforded such an expensive wedding? Was it entirely due to the Watson-Fanshaw Detective Agency, or was 'Hugh Boone' up to some new game in the begging line well outside London, and away from the sharp eyes of Inspector Bradstreet?

"What is it Sherlock wants?" I asked warily as Emily and I walked slowly down the steps of St. George's and watched the young people throwing rice over the bride and bridegroom.

"Patience, Muriel," she said, using the old name Moriarty had given me when he hoped I would become one of his agents. A name she liked to roll round her tongue whenever she felt like reminding me how nearly I had fallen into the man's clutches at the beginning of *The Sign of Fear*. "We have the Reception to get through. I only hope Mr. St. Clair has his speech ready."

"And that the groomsman's isn't too near the knuckle," I said with a grin.

"I really believe you are trying to ruin my lovely day with such an outrageous suggestion," she said, dabbing her

102

dry eyes with the corner of a dry handkerchief. "But it's true I shall have to watch him. He is too much given to reading *The Idler*."

"That reminds me of several other mass-circulation magazines," I said. "I wonder if you remember Beeton's *Christmas Annual*?"

"I remember you telling me once that you had nothing to do with what went into that particular organ. Said it was before your time. By which I presumed you meant before you met that husband of yours."

"But did you ever read that thing Sherlock, John and Arthur concocted between them, 'A Study in Scarlet'?"

"Yes," said Emily, "and there were certain things in it I considered decidedly odd."

"Tell me more," I said eagerly, anxious to hear anything which might make Holmes look silly, and not at all worried about who knew my feelings on the subject.

"To begin with, why was the German word for revenge – *rache* – written on the wall of that house in Brixton? *And* in the hotel bedroom where Stangerson was stabbed to death? Jefferson Hope was an American."

"Both strange and dramatic. A good touch to any tale. But, in my considered opinion, Holmes chose to use the word so that Inspector Lestrade could seem to cloud the issue, increase the mystery and finally be made to look stupid by suggesting it was the beginning of a girl's name."

"Look foolish in the light of later events you mean?"

"Not at all," I said. "Sherlock Holmes enlightened Lestrade before everybody left Lauriston Gardens. But one must remember that the policeman had certain disadvantages. He didn't speak the language and had probably never been to Heidelberg. Or even heard of it."

"Heidelberg? What's Heidelberg got to do with it?"

"The word RACHE is scratched on a wall in the students' jail there."

"Students' jail?" Emily was beginning to sound more and more like an angry parrot.

"If one of the youths attending the University gets into trouble with the Civil Authorities or, come to that, his tutor it's left to the College to punish him."

"By making him take part in a sword fight?" I've heard all about those 'honourable' duelling scars," said Emily with relish.

"By putting him in a cell for a certain period, depending on the severity of his 'crime'."

"So is that where Mr. Holmes got the idea for the murderer writing 'revenge' in a foreign language? Do you think *he* was ever in Heidelberg?"

"Sherlock?" I asked. "Either that, or he was fond of reading the travel books written by a certain very well-known American author!"

"Well I never. Who'd have thought it? After all that man said to your husband about storing only useful things in one's little attic of a brain."

"It did come in useful," I said dryly. "Twice. Once in Lauriston Gardens and again at Halliday's Private Hotel. But I hardly think that would be of interest now."

A few days later, when the Watson family were at breakfast and Nip was trying to decide between another piece of toast and a third slice of bacon, there was a loud rat-tat at the front door. Shortly afterwards a servant brought in a large envelope addressed to the Watson-Fanshaw Detective Agency.

"My, that's an impressive looking epistle," whistled John, pouring himself a second cup of tea. "As I once said to Holmes. It was a few weeks before we married, my dear, while I was still living in Baker Street. Sherlock, being the man he was, started looking in a big red book and read out a description of the coat of arms on the back of the envelope. 'Azure: three caltrops in chief over a fess sable'."

"Caltrops? In chief? Fess?" asked Nip indistinctly through a large mouthful of toast. "Azure?" He had a book propped up in front of him while he ate his breakfast, preparing for an algebra test later that morning.

"Iron balls with four spikes," said John. "'In chief' means the top third of a shield, and the fess – in this case black – is a horizontal band which separates the caltrops (sometimes called calthropes or carltraps) from the lower two thirds. Azure, of course, is the overall colour of this particular accoutrement."

"If I finish my test early, I'll make a drawing of the whole silly thing," said Nip.

"Mind you get it right, for the honour of the Watsons," said John jovially.

"Who haven't got a coat of arms!"

"Not yet," I said, secretly wondering what my dear friend Emily would have made of all this erudition, especially so early in the morning. If she were with us she would be sharpening her wits in order to deliver her usual heavy sarcasms on the subject of 'useless knowledge', especially poor Watson's. Aloud I said, remembering all that writing Sherlock had done for *The Strand Magazine* (while passing it off as an old soldier's), "A little bit of space-filling as usual. The Balmorals seem a blood-thirsty lot, putting those horrible iron things on their shields."

"It's to show how far back they go as members of the Aristocracy," said John through a mouthful of muffin. "Caltrops are very ancient symbols. All those border raids and such. The spiky balls are probably a reminder of the ones their ancestors threw down in order to impede enemy horses busy chasing after them. Having a spike positioned on every side…"

"Round objects don't have sides," said Nip.

"No. But they roll," said his father grimly. "Which must have some significance!"

"Well, never mind that now," I said, slitting open my letter. The coat of arms on it was much more elaborate than the one belonging to Lord St. Simon's family, the man Holmes called 'The Noble Bachelor'. A Double-Headed Eagle for Germany, a Cardinal's Red Hat for Spain – now how on earth had that got into anyone's ancestry? – impaled with the Arms of the person Watson told me was The Duke of Lomond. Whose Family Motto was 'Still Waters Run Deep,'

"Very appropriate to both of them," murmured John. "He because of his Scottish Estates near the famous Loch, and her…"

"Isadora Klein, the widow of the Sugar King?" I said. "It was in all the papers that she had married as her second husband a boy almost young enough to be her son. I wonder the Family stood for it."

"She's enormously rich," said Watson. "So that probably helped matters. But what does she want?"

"She doesn't deign to say. Simply summons us to Grosvenor Square for eleven o'clock. Nip, ring the bell for a servant to clear the table and, Watson, put through a telephone call to Mrs. St. Clair to come round as soon as possible in a cab."

"I'll tell her to forget the trousers, shall I?"

"I should say so. A decent frock is what's wanted on this occasion. Not too elaborate. We don't need to risk putting the Duchess in the shade."

"That would be difficult. She's one of the world's most beautiful women by all accounts."

"But getting a bit long in the tooth."

"I always thought Emily was the catty one," said John, making hastily for the hall, where the telephone was kept hidden behind a pot plant similar to the aspidistra Moriarty's minions asked me to put in the window whenever Watson was away and I was available to work for him.

I was glad to see Miss Fanshaw, properly dressed for once, arrive at our house in Kensington in good time. She was highly excited by the idea of visiting a member of the Aristocracy, however dubious her reputation, and also liked the fact that the prospective client was fabulously rich. This should mean a hefty fee as soon as she – we – had discovered what there was to do. And hadn't Mr. Sherlock Holmes once got five thousand pounds out of the woman with very little effort at the end of the investigation into what he called 'The Adventure of The Three Gables'?

The house when we reached it proved to be one of the finest dwellings in the West End of London. As we went up the steps I saw Emily adjusting her dress, her parasol and her expression. So even she was overcome by the magnificence of her surroundings. Just as I was by the magnificence of the footman who opened the door to our knock. Her Grace was expecting us, he said, and we were led into a room of fantastic proportions – but with very little illumination. What had Watson said when he first met the woman? "The lady had come, I felt, to that time of life when even the proudest beauty finds the half light more welcome."

"Candles," hissed Mrs. St. Clair gleefully in my ear. "Always more flattering to the older woman."

But the Duchess of Lomond was still rather wonderful. Tall, queenly, with a perfect figure, a lovely mask-like face and two magnificent Spanish eyes, I couldn't help speculating on what she must have been like in her heyday. Waving an imperious hand, she motioned to us to sit down and came straight to the point. "My husband," she said, "has vanished."

"When and where?" asked Emily briskly, at the same time producing her note book.

"Two days ago. And if I knew where I wouldn't have to bother with two female detectives."

"I mean," said Miss Fanshaw tartly, "where from, not where is he."

"From this house. Immediately after breakfast." It was obvious she disliked all other women, and I guessed it was only our growing reputation which had caused her to decide on consulting the Watson-Fanshaw Detective Agency in preference to any similar organisation staffed by men.

"Perhaps the Duke had important business on hand," I said in a voice meant to be placating.

"What, on the eve of the most magnificent Ball of the Season? One which was due to be held here, and to which everyone of any importance had been invited? Besides, he did not return, as he must have done if it was only a matter of business."

"And the dance was cancelled?"

"Certainly not. It was far too important. Fortunately, His Grace's uncle was able to support me and I could at least enter the Supper Room on an unattached gentleman's arm."

A doddering old scion of an ancient house, almost ready for the bone yard and with a terrible reputation as an out and out roué. But, looking on the bright side, the Duchess was probably quite glad to have him as a partner. It could only point up her beauty, however much that might have diminished since the days of her splendid youth.

"So you have no idea where your husband has gone and why he has vanished," said Emily, cutting into my thoughts.

"None whatsoever," said the Duchess with a frown.

"Not kidnapped for a ransom?"

"I'm the one with the money," retorted the woman, showing how ill-bred she really was. "Left to me as the widow of Herr Klein. Any crooks would be better off kidnapping me. The Lomonds have hardly a penny to bless themselves with."

"So that's why they welcomed the woman into the fold," said Emily, giving the handsome footman a flirtatious look before tripping down the front steps of the house twirling her parasol. "Well, we will have to do our best to find the young man."

"And screw as much out of madam as we can when we do."

"It beats me why she wants to get him back. After all, she has the house and everything –and can still call herself a Duchess."

"The one thing these famous beauties can't abide is being deserted by someone," I said. "If it is done they like to be the ones to do it. Besides, if the Duke is not found within a certain time and presumed dead the heir to the title may decide to chuck her out. Of course, she would still have enough money to support herself in luxury. But her social position might be up the spout."

"What very peculiar expressions you do use," said Mrs. St. Clair, forgetting some of her own efforts in that direction, when she could be as coarse as any Billingsgate fishwife.

It was while we were walking away from the house towards a cab rank that Emily and I were nearly run down by a Grosvenor Square furniture van careering madly along the road and almost mounting the pavement. Just as we were shaking our fists at the driver a small and very hard object hit my colleague in the face, causing her to curse loudly and drop the precious parasol. The very one she had ordered for Grizelda's wedding.

As Emily was ruefully rubbing her cheek, I bent down to retrieve the offending object. To my surprise it was a dried pea. "Here we are in the most expensive area of Town," I said wonderingly, "and someone is using a peashooter."

"A what?" she spat out, dabbing the wound carefully with a lace handkerchief to see how much blood there was.

"A narrow metal tube young ruffians employ to aim peas at people. They think it's fun."

"I'll give them fun," said Miss Fanshaw. She hailed a growler, leapt into it (at the same time pulling me very roughly inside by the wrist) and ordered the driver to chase every furniture van he could see. Of course it was useless. The speed 'our' van had been going, it was already out of sight: and there were no others in the immediate vicinity. Emily banged angrily on the roof of the vehicle and ordered the man to take us to 'The Laurels'. Once there, she changed rapidly into male attire, called for her own carriage and, with me inside it, mounted on the box with a muttered oath. She then drove madly down the Bayswater Road as if all the fiends of hell were after her.

The way she whipped up her horses left me wondering how long it would be before we overturned. And if we didn't, how the wretched animals would be able to stand the pace. Or if I would ever see my home, husband and child again. But I kept my eyes tightly closed during the nightmare ride and so was surprised, when she finally stopped, to find myself once more in Grosvenor Square. Emily put her head through the window and said with a wolfish grin, "If that rat of a pea-shooting blackguard delivered furniture here once he'll do it again. Then we'll see how this ancient blunderbuss suits him."

"Any fresh furniture items may not be delivered by the same person," I protested in a horrified voice.

"So what? News will get back to the warehouse and frighten the life out of whoever actually did the deed."

Although the pea must have stung her badly I couldn't help feeling the reaction was out of all proportion to the offence, and was about to enlarge on this when an old gentleman walking across the Square suddenly leapt in the air with an anguished cry and began rubbing an unmentionable part of his person, the part where the jacket meets the nether garment. At that precise moment a furniture van labelled with the letters 'Moving is our Metier' shot out of an area and careered wildly in the direction of Brook Street – its wheels, as before, almost mounting the pavement, and with a fine disregard for any unwary pedestrians.

Emily was up on the box again in a flash and, belabouring her animals more than ever, swung her vehicle round so that it blocked the van's exit from the Square. I sprang out of my seat, ran past the heads of the sweating horses and said in a loud voice, "Look! The thing's empty. The back doors are open. And that young man inside, who's up on one knee with the peashooter in his fist, is the missing Duke of Lomond."

"Well, he wasn't so far away from his own property," she said wonderingly, covering the miscreant with her blunderbuss. "But what about the driver?"

"Wiggins, by all that's wonderful!" I said.

"Yuss," said that gentleman gruffly, at the same time fingering a tattered neckerchief, "the bloke your husband once called 'insignificant and unsavoury'!"

"That was before he really knew you," I said hastily.

"But I must say you do get in with some very queer folks yourself, Mrs. Watson," said the young gentleman, eyeing the blunderbuss warily. "I hope you realise I'm only the reluctant dogsbody."

"Dogsbody be blowed, Wiggo," said Emily, who had met the boy when we were on the track of the felonious Master of Corpus Christi College, Cambridge in *A Study in Crimson*.

By this time his companion had climbed out of the back of the van and said in a cultured voice, "You mustn't blame Wiggo. That is, I mean Mr. Wiggins. I haven't had such a jolly time in years."

"Jolly for you maybe," said Mrs. St. Clair, with a baleful glance at the peashooter. "What about that poor wife of yours pining for you at home?"

"If she's doing that, she's a changed woman," said the Duke. "All that person cares about is my title. Have you any idea how awful it is to be married to someone almost old enough to be your mother and who, in spite of all that cash, keeps one short of pocket money as if one were nothing but a naughty school-boy? I even had to tie the knot in a dark old church in Spanish Place lit only by guttering candles. It made me thoroughly miserable."

"Yuss," said Wiggins again suddenly. "Anyone with 'arf an 'eart would be right sorry for 'im."

"That's right," said Lomond happily. "So much so, I'm going to live with Mr. Wiggins in Camberwell."

"Me and Alf both," cut in Wiggins.

"Of course," carolled the Duke. "You *and* Alf."

"He has some queer habits," I said.

"Not these days 'e 'asn't," replied Wiggins.

"No more stalking, jumping out at h'innocent young females and setting fire to fings for 'im – such as you mentioned in your larst book. The Duke here has given us some of his old duds. At least they're supposed to be his old clothes, although blokes like me and Alf would never think it, and we go swaggering down the Strand like a couple of Lords of Creation."

"That's all very well," said Miss Fanshaw suddenly. "But if I hear of any more peas being shot all over the place you'll have me to deal with." And she waved the blunderbuss in their faces with a most menacing air.

"These things are fun to begin with," said the young Duke of Lomond hastily, meaning pea-shooters.. "But of course they're inclined to pall after a while."

"And we do have all this furniture to collect and deliver," said the driver. "Cos that's wot pays the rent."

"How did you recognise the Duke of Lomond so easily?" asked Emily once we had returned exhausted to 'The Laurels', given the carriage and horses over to the stable boy and settled down to a good gossip.

"*The Strand Magazine* periodically publishes pages of photographs of prominent people, from birth to their present more mature age."

"But surely the Duke of Lomond is far too young for that?"

"The article I saw was about His Grace the former Duke, a Colonial Potentate of some kind. Our Duke was in one of the photographs with his father."

"Well that was a piece of luck," said Emily from behind the teapot. "Personally I never read the rag. Neville won't have it in the house. Says it's for young city clerks, as I believe your husband mentioned once."

"One can't be picky," I said, helping myself to a ratafia biscuit. "Not, that is, if one wants to be a successful detective. All means of gathering information must be explored. Look at Sherlock Holmes and his 'great index volumes with the records of old cases, mixed with the accumulated information of a lifetime.'"

"That's what he led us all to believe; and I never thought I'd hear you hold up that gentleman as a shining example of anything," said Mrs. St. Clair, grabbing a biscuit in her turn. "And as for that ridiculous story about a Sussex Vampire...Do you remember telling me in the train to Greenport, Long Island that if he hadn't deliberately muddled up dates and whatnot it would have been much easier to discover what he was really up to? Take that affair of the blanched soldier, for example."

"The story Sherlock actually admitted writing himself?"

"And said it was a real investigation."

"I know exactly what you are going to say," I said, holding out my cup for more tea. "Mr. Sherlock Holmes completely forgot his account of something he called 'The Priory School', and when that investigation was supposed to have happened. By the time he wrote about pseudo-leprosy in 'The Blanched Soldier' the Priory School had become The Abbey School, The Duke of Holdernesse The Duke of Greyminster and the time two years later!"

"I must say you look very pleased about it," said Mrs. St. Clair. "Something which I find somewhat surprising, considering the outrageous statement he made right at the beginning of all that nonsense."

"'The good Watson had at that time deserted me for a wife', you mean? You'd never believe the amount of speculation that has caused. Was she The Gold King Neil Gibson's children's governess, a woman of the streets called Kitty Winter – or even the wayward girl that the so-called illustrious client interested himself in? John's been teasing me about it on and off for years."

"If I remember rightly, you were also 'killed off' earlier in one of those fantastic flights of fancy."

"Yes," I said, wondering how she knew all this if copies of *The Strand Magazine,* 'that rag' as she called it, weren't allowed inside 'The Laurels'. "As an alternative to appearing in what were supposed to be his narratives of real investigations, Watson suggested I retire to an out of the way place in Yorkshire called Masongill. To look after Arthur's mother, if you please. That's when I decided to open a detective agency."

But Emily had lost interest and asked, "Do you think we're likely to be paid for this latest fiasco?"

I told her that this highly *unlikely* and, in order to prevent her from losing her temper and smashing a teacup, said that in any case we had done very little. Her answer to this was that she didn't think dashing round London, driving her own carriage and lathering her horses, was very little; and, as in the past, it had prevented us from investigating what could have been more lucrative problems.

"Sherlock said the game was the thing, not the money."

"A fat lot of investigating he did by all accounts," said Emily Fanshaw vulgarly. "Surely you're not about to form a one-woman Admiration Society for the man? That would certainly be a turn up for the book!"

The day after this barbed chat with my comrade-in-arms I wrote a letter on behalf of the Watson-Fanshaw Detective Agency to the Duchess of Lomond telling her that, although we had found the Duke, there was no prospect of her ever getting her husband back under the marital roof. It was up to her what she did next; and I didn't mention the possibility of any payment for our services, such as they were.

A week later a letter with a Camberwell postmark arrived by district messenger to say that His Grace intended to give up his title and all that went with it. At the same time he was seeking an Annulment of his Union with the woman Miss Fanshaw had started to call the Merry Widow: although I for one failed to grasp what was jovial about her. If the arrangement with Wiggins and his friend Alf failed, he would happily go to sea as a deck hand. When I telephoned Mrs. St. Clair with this news all she said was that if the furniture van continued in the Grosvenor Square area the Duchess would one day come down the steps of her magnificent mansion, spot her erring spouse and grab him warmly by the throat.

"But it's more likely," I said, "that those two characters will begin delivering their goods in another part of the Metropolis to avoid such a *contretemps*. Especially after seeing us there as well."

"Let's hope it's not Whitechapel then," said the disembodied voice. "Where nobody has the money for new beds. Or, indeed, any beds at all: and, if they don't sit on the floor, have only an upturned beer barrel to accommodate them."

I asked her what she thought would happen to Isadora Klein if the Duke's plans went ahead. "She'll probably marry that old roué the young man's uncle, after she's certain he will succeed to the title, and serve her right."

117

Putting my private opinions on hold, I reluctantly asked Emily if it meant that now at last we had to get in touch with Holmes? I left her promising to find out exactly what my not-so-favourite sleuth (the supposedly retired same) might want, while I went looking for John to ask whether the subject of wills had ever come up during his time in Baker Street. As it turned out, Sir James Damery wasn't concerned in the matter at all. The soporific air of the Sussex seaside, combined with the loss of his precious monographs, was obviously causing Sherlock to lose his famous acumen; and when Miss Fanshaw appeared on the doorstep a few days later, with a very tiny woman wearing fingerless black mittens and carrying an umbrella exactly like Sarah Gamp's in tow, she told me Holmes had solved the Hammerford Will case and was no longer in need of our services.

"Solved it no doubt by sitting up all night on a pile of cushions smoking a horrible brand of shag tobacco," I said sourly. "Meanwhile surrounding himself with disgusting dottles. If indeed there ever was such a case."

But it meant the man was out of our hair, at least for the time being. For which I, for one, was extremely grateful. The thought of Mrs. St. Clair re-playing her school girl role in front of Sherlock, if he had engaged us, was guaranteed to make me as cross as two sticks. It would be worse than putting up with Isadora Klein's arrogant ways. Mrs St. Clair, however, was anxious to come into the house and, once there, began helping our visitor off with her bonnet and shawl. "This is Matilda Clutterbuck," she said, at the same time hiding a smirk behind her hand, "who has expressed a wish to consult us about a disappearing husband."

Surely not another one? Absent husbands were becoming very prevalent it seemed, and in danger of being something of a disease. I almost felt Emily had brought the queer little creature to me on purpose. I put the old woman at her ease, however, by installing her in a capacious armchair (which almost swallowed her up) and rang for a servant to bring in some tea. Glaring balefully at Miss Fanshaw, I reluctantly settled down to listen to another tale of matrimonial mayhem. After all, shouldn't the Watson-Fanshaw Agency be ready to deal with anything, however repetitious?

A FRAGMENT

One bitterly cold evening, when the wind howled even more dolorously than usual outside the window of our rooms in Baker Street, Holmes suddenly sat up in his armchair and remarked in a self-satisfied voice, "The trousers of course. What else could it be but the trousers?"

He had been sitting opposite me for a considerable time in complete silence, broken only by the sound of a roaring fire crackling cheerfully in the grate, and it was with some surprise that I now looked enquiringly at him over the top of my newspaper.

"You remember, my dear fellow, that little affair in Bermondsey, where a certain gentleman of our acquaintance had no idea what had happened to his nether garment? Something which, for a time at least, caused him considerable distress before it was found in the place he least expected it to be, and where he had so decidedly omitted to look?

"I can't say I do," I replied cautiously. "Besides, aren't you engaged at present on a far more important case than any involving a man's sartorial attire?"

"Yes," replied Sherlock Holmes impatiently, suddenly getting to his feet to extract a spill from the box on the mantelpiece and poking it into the flames to relight his cherrywood pipe. "But don't you see how deductions arrived at by studying something as simple as mislaying a pair of trousers can be equally useful when it comes to a far more important matter. The loss of the Rajah's Scarab for example?"

Well now at least I understood his reference to trousers. But, although I knew he had been investigating the Rajah's problem for some days, I also knew from Holmes' manner there was nothing more to be done about it at present. That, and the way such a gale was blowing outside. When I mentioned this latter point, however, he said through a cloud of smoke,

"Nonsense, Doctor. With your help, I'll solve it sitting here - while the wind can do what it likes."

I was somewhat taken aback by the suggestion that I could be of help in a matter of which I knew next to nothing.

"But," said Holmes, "A friend is always useful…"

As a sounding board, of course! Someone who would happily sit by and pay close attention while he sorted out his thoughts. I say 'happily' because it had always been my pleasure, indeed privilege, to listen to his astounding theories – and perhaps add a little something of my own. Which is why I normally raised no objections whenever he needed to discuss a case. Although I must confess that I often felt he was talking more to himself than to me.

"It is my opinion that the Rajah has at least two scarabs," said Holmes, stretching out his thin legs before the fire.

"Considering the extreme wealth of these Potentates he probably has more than he, or his minions, can count."

"But one of them is particularly special?"

"Watson, I have already said I believe he has two very special jewels. There is no doubt in my mind that they are identical, and of immense and equal value. But he is convinced that one of them has been stolen."

"And you are not?"

"It is by no means certain; and if I may return to the matter of the trousers for a moment I will tell you why."

It was at that precise point that I realised my slippers were in danger of getting scorched and jumped up hastily to move my armchair a little away from the hearth. Holmes, however, misjudged the movement and said testily, "Oh well, if you're not particularly interested…"

"Of course I'm interested," I said crossly."But you can't expect complete concentration from a fellow whose foot feels as if it's about to catch fire."

"My dear chap, accept my most sincere apologies," said my friend with a laugh, waving his pipe in the air and appearing more cheerful than he had all evening. "Sit down again while I explain my reasoning. It's like this: the Rajah, as I believe was his wont whenever he had a suitable visitor, used to send for the two jewels in order to show them off to someone not quite as wealthy as he is. When he came to England with his entourage a few months ago he continued the habit, having brought the scarabs with him, and now one of them is missing."

"And the other?"

"Stowed away in a safe at the Northumberland Hotel."…

LOG-ROLLING

This expression, which originated in America during the old pioneering days, when one settler helped another to clear a patch in the forest for a cabin and expected the same help in return, later became attached to books. 'Literary Log-rolling' involves writing a fulsome review of a fellow-author's novel in the expectation that he or she will do the same for you.

Ada Levison, a great friend of Somerset Maugham and also a writer, contacted 'The Academy', a Journal edited by Oscar Wilde's lover Lord Alfred Douglas, saying she very much wanted to write a review of a play by Maugham. Douglas agreed, provided there was "no log-rolling."[1] In the event, he returned the review as "much too obviously a 'puff'," at the same time saying "If Maugham was so anxious to meet me it is a pity he did not do so before I became Editor of a paper which is capable of being very useful to him."[2]

Conan Doyle is said to have arranged for friends to puff his books, and is known to have placed advertisements in several newspapers about them, in the same way as he made sure his attendance at accidents was fully reported when he was a struggling young doctor in Southsea.[3] So the process (still taking place today) has been well-known and popular for many years. And, presumably, works.

1 See *Brewer's Dictionary of Phrase and Fable* 1894:768

[2]Quoted in *The Secret Lives of Somerset Maugham* by Selina Hastings

[3]See *A Study in Southsea* by Geoffrey Stavert

"ONCE ABOARD THE LUGGER..."

Before graduating from Edinburgh University and putting up his plate in Southsea, Conan Doyle went as a nominal surgeon on a seven-month voyage to the Arctic and his description (in 'The Captain of the Polestar') of a burial at sea is so vivid that he might almost have witnessed one for himself on board the whaler. Later, soon after he had passed his examinations, he sailed on a cargo-and-passenger-liner to the West Coast of Africa as a fully qualified ship's surgeon and wrote several short stories based on these experiences. They included 'Habakuk Jephson's Statement', an original and highly imaginative 'solution' to the mystery of the *Marie Celeste.*

When he became famous these stories were hunted down in various magazines and rapidly re-published in book form. 'Tales of Pirates' and 'Tales of Blue Water' (in which both the Habakuk and the Polestar stories appear, together with the exploits of Captain Starkey) were closely followed by 'Tales of the Ring and the Camp', 'Tales of

Terror and Mystery', 'Tales of Twilight and the Unseen' 'Tales of Adventure and Medical Life' and 'Tales of Long Ago' – all published, for example, in John Murray's Fiction Library of Two-Shilling Novels. One can only marvel at the creative energy which produced all this, along with the Historical Novels, 'Uncle Bernac', the Brigadier Gerard books, A History of the Boer War and, of course, Sherlock Holmes!

Mention of Murray recalls a certain passage in Habakuk, where the writer takes part in the American Civil War and says, "I was severely wounded at Antietam, and would probably have perished on the field if it had not been for the kindness of a gentleman named Murray, who had me carried to his house and provided me with every comfort."

A passage which must find an echo with everyone who has ever read Doctor Watson's account of his experiences at the Battle of Maiwand in 'A Study in Scarlet'.

ARTHUR AND BEATRIX

In 1901, at the age of 35, Beatrix Potter produced her first book for children. It was called *The Tale of Peter Rabbit* and she sent it, unsuccessfully, to Frederick Warne & Co. Ltd. Six more publishers also refused it. So Miss Potter decided to publish the book herself. She brought out a limited edition of 250 copies, made up by someone introduced to her by the daughter of the editor of *The Geological Magazine*. "Who," she said, "knew something of printing and engraving."

The little book did so well among relatives and friends that the author decided to approach Warne's again. After all, "They had written that they were pleased with the designs and were the only firm that had softened a refusal with expressions of polite interest." Letters went back and forth from Bolton Gardens (where the Potter family lived) to Bedford Street where Warne's had its offices, and the upshot of it all was that the firm finally decided to publish if the black and white drawings were replaced by coloured plates.

Rather artlessly, perhaps, Miss Potter had written in one of her letters "I do not know if it is worth mentioning but Dr. Conan Doyle had a copy for his children, and he has a good opinion of the story and words." Doyle had by this time moved from South Norwood to Hindhead and it isn't easy to see how he got to know about the book and managed to buy it. He was, however, becoming very well known through the stories he wrote for *The Strand Magazine*; and Beatrix had so many relatives and friends to whom she was selling her book the chances were that a copy eventually got to him through one of them.

His children at that time were Mary, aged 12, and Kingsley, aged nine. The thought occurs that they were maybe a little too old for *Peter*. But children in those days grew up more slowly than they do now, and the coloured plates were superb. Although the animals are, in some instances, anthropomorphically dressed in clothes, they remain in essentials entirely true to themselves. Peter, for example, steals lettuces and runs away on all fours (and in an abject state of terror) from an irate farmer. And at no time does he cease to look anything other than a real rabbit.

ARTHUR AND PLUM

'"You watch that pig of yours like a hawk, Clarence, or before you know where you are, this fiend in human shape will be slipping pineapple bombs into her bran mash." The words had sunk in, as such words would scarcely have failed to do, and they caused Lord Emsworth to entertain towards Sir Gregory feelings similar to, though less cordial than, those of Sherlock Holmes towards Moriarty.'

This reference to Sherlock Holmes in *Pigs Have Wings* by P. G. Wodehouse (generally known to his chums as 'Plum') is one of a great many scattered throughout his books: "Come Watson, come, the game is afoot." "You know my methods. Apply them." "Did you ever read *The Hound of the Baskervilles*? That bit where Holmes and Watson are lurking in the mist..." There's mention of Chicago gangsters, and the Earl of Ickenham has Altamont as one of his names.

In *The Code of the Woosters,* Bertie (already alarmed by the unexpected arrival of the arch-snooper Roderick Spode) is ordered by his Aunt Dahlia to steal a silver cow-creamer and says feelingly, "Imagine how some Master Criminal would feel on coming down to do a murder at the old Grange if he found Sherlock Holmes putting in the weekend there."

The question is, why should Holmes be mentioned so many times? Indeed, why should he be mentioned at all?

It doesn't seem to be simply 'literary log rolling' since, although the two authors were friends and played cricket together, there's no record of Doyle including any of Wodehouse's characters in his tales! But, of course, both wrote for *The Strand Magazine.*

In *Service with a Smile* one reads, "Beyond the obvious facts that the miscreant was a Freemason, left-handed, chewed tobacco and had travelled in the east..." This, being a typical Holmsian moment from somebody in the tale who is hardly a detective at all but a scheming little boy, adds even more humour to an already comic situation: especially as so many of the people in Wodehouse's stories love scenting mysteries and spend all their time sorting them out. Readers familiar with Holmes' milieu will give a complicit grin at this copying of his style of speech. After all, didn't Sherlock say of the pawnbroker Jabez Wilson, in 'The Red-Headed League', "Beyond the obvious facts that he has at some time done manual labour, that he takes snuff, that he is a Freemason, that he has been in China, and that he has done a considerable amount of writing lately..."

THE MAIWAND LION

This tribute to the men of The 66th Regiment of Foot ("The Royal Berkshires") stands in Forbury Gardens, Reading. At the time of the Battle of Maiwand in late July, 1880 the momentum for erecting such memorials was somewhat rare. But defeat was so unexpected, total and out of the ordinary, and the Last Stand of the remnants of the Regiment so captured the imagination of the British public, that it was decided to commission George Simonds, an eminent sculptor with strong local connections since his family owned Simonds Brewery, to provide something fitting.

He decided on a cast-iron lion standing on a pedestal – which would have the names of 328 commissioned and, unusually for those days, non-commissioned men inscribed on it. After this was agreed to, Simonds spent some time in London Zoo, studying the lions there and finally producing something which could be thought to represent the lion-hearted courage of the doomed soldiers, as well as the snarling and majestic might of the British Empire.

SPOT THE CHANGES

There are several differences between this drawing and the one on page 9. Can you spot them all?

'Sheerluck Homes' and
'Dr. Spotson' as they appeared in
'The Magnet' No.1651 vol LVl
w/e Oct. 7th 1939

YOU'VE READ THE BOOK. NOW TRY THE
QUIZ!

http://www.surveymonkey.com/s/KD2R8XT

Also from Molly Carr

The first two adventures in the Watson and Fanshaw
detective series.

*"What we have here is no more or less than a gorgeous
romp involving several characters from the Holmes Canon,
principally Mary Watson. The action flows along with great
humour (very often at Watson's expense) and verve. A
rollercoaster of a novel with gear changes a plenty (in
more ways than one!), a delicious turn of phrase on
occasion, a whiff of sexuality and a fabulously drawn
central character in Mary Watson. You will never think of
Watson's wife in the same vein again. Highly
recommended."* **Effortless Enigma**

Also from Molly Carr

The definitive biography of Dr. Watson, now in its extended and
revised second edition.

Also from Molly Carr

"Who were PC Pollack, and Dr Ferrier? Who lived in Potter's Terrace, and who went to Eton? What were Poncho and Pugilist? Molly Carr could justifiably have called her remarkably comprehensive new book: A Sherlock Holmes Who's Who, Where's Where, and What's What. The information provided for each entry is concise and helpful. This Who's Who may not aim to compete with Jack Tracy's all-but-definitive Encyclopaedia Sherlockiana, but it is a very useful reference resource, one which, I fancy, I shall consult frequently".

Sherlock Holmes Society of London

Also from MX Publishing

MX Publishing is proud to support the campaign to save and restore Sir Arthur Conan Doyle's former home. Undershaw is where he brought Sherlock Holmes back to life, and should be preserved for future generations of Holmes fans.

Save Undershaw   www.saveundershaw.com

Facebook   www.facebook.com/saveundershaw

You can read more about Sir Arthur Conan Doyle and Undershaw in Alistair Duncan's book (share of royalties to the Undershaw Preservation Trust) – An Entirely New Country and in the amazing compilation Sherlock's Home – The Empty House (all royalties to the Trust).

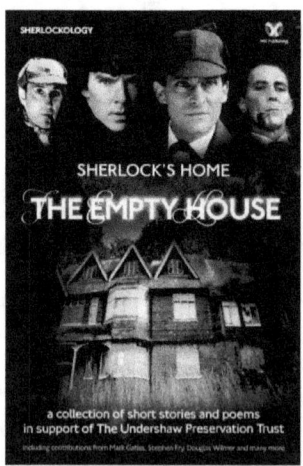 

Also from MX Publishing

Sherlock Holmes Travel Guides

In ebook an interactive guide to London

400 locations linked to Google Street View.

Also from MX Publishing

Cross over fiction featuring great villans from history

  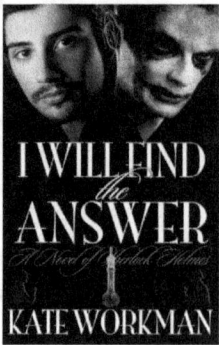

Fantasy Sherlock Holmes

www.mxpublishing.com

From one of the world's largest Sherlock Holmes publishers dozens of new novels from the top Holmes authors – including Alistair Duncan Winner of the 2011 Howlett Literary Award (Sherlock Holmes book of the year) for 'The Norwood Author'

www.mxpublishing.com

New in 2012 [Novels unless stated]:

Sherlock Holmes and the Plague of Dracula
Sherlock Holmes and The Adventure of The Jacobite Rose [Play]
Sherlock Holmes and The Whitechapel Vampire
Holmes Sweet Holmes
The Detective and The Woman: A Novel of Sherlock Holmes
Sherlock Holmes Tales From The Stranger's Room
The Sherlock Holmes Who's Who [Reference]
Sherlock Holmes and The Dead Boer at Scotney Castle
The Secret Journal of Dr Watson
A Professor Reflects on Sherlock Holmes [Essay Collection]
Sherlock Holmes of The Lyme Regis Legacy
Sherlock Holmes and The Discarded Cigarette [Short Novel]
Sherlock Holmes On The Air [Radio Plays]
Sherlock Holmes and The Murder at Lodore Falls

Untold Adventure of Sherlock Holmes
The Many Watsons [review of actors]
Sherlock Holmes and The Case of The Crystal Blue Bottle
[Graphic Novel]
Sherlock Holmes and The Missing Snowman [Children's
Book]

Also from Kieran McMullen

"Few people have considered the early life of John H Watson in any depth. Kieran McMullen, author of Watson's Afghan Adventure is a former professional soldier and a specialist in American military history an appropriate person to tell of Watson s experiences as an army surgeon. Exciting, and full of authentic military detail."

Sherlock Holmes Society of London

www.ingramcontent.com/pod-product-compliance
Lightning Source LLC
Chambersburg PA
CBHW071312130626
46556CB00004B/1579